BREWIN' UP LOVE
THE COFFEE LOFT

KACI LANE

Copyright © 2024 by Kaci Lane

All rights reserved.

This is a work of fiction. Names, characters, organizations, places, events and incidents are either products of the author's imagination or are used fictitiously. Any resemblance to actual persons, living or dead, or actual events is purely coincidental.

No part of this work may be reproduced, or stored in a retrieval system, or transmitted in any form by any means without written permission from the author.

*To my friend and fellow author, Ginny Sterling.
Thanks for asking "again" if I'd like to join this series. It's what I
needed right now.
Love you!*

BREWIN' UP LOVE

CHAPTER 1

Brooke

"One lava cake with ice cream." The waitress smiles.

My eyes widen as she slides a large plate of chocolatey goodness in front of Nate and me. I unfold a paper napkin and tuck the end in the neck of my dress. Mama will have my hide if I stain my prom dress with syrup. Nate rolls up his sleeves, but doesn't show much concern. He shovels in a big bite, taking out half the whipped cream topping.

A few more of our friends order dessert, and Jonah asks for another refill of tea. Nate suggested we go someplace really upscale, but I didn't want him to waste money when I eat chicken most everywhere we go. Applebee's with our friends is perfectly fine by me, especially when he wouldn't dare let me help pay.

Our entire relationship, he's treated me like a queen. I could easily pay for anything we do, but I don't want to embarrass him. Nate is the type who wants to take care of everyone, including himself.

I take a small bite of cake and ice cream, careful to lean over the plate. The other girls eating desserts take their time as well. Nate quickly eats most of our shared dessert, leaving little for me to worry about falling on my dress. Most people with his appetite would be overweight, but most of them don't play ball all the time.

He had some kind of practice game or tournament this morning. I couldn't go, because it conflicted with my hair appointment.

The waitress comes back with checks and asks if anyone needs a to-go box. I stare at the stained-glass lighting above the bar and fight the emotions welling inside me.

Tonight is our prom. Senior prom.

The guys played their last high school baseball game a few weeks ago, and I finished cheer months back. Prom is our last stop before graduation.

Nate's hand lands on my bare shoulders, bringing a comforting warmth. "You okay?"

I nod and force a smile. "I just can't believe how fast this year has gone."

"But we've got the rest of our lives ahead of us." He smiles.

My shoulders untense and I relax against his arm. He has a natural way of putting me at ease.

"It's here." Carolina perks up and lifts her phone. Everyone stares at her in confusion, including her date.

"My surprise." She throws up a hand, as if that clarifies anything.

We continue staring. She stands and wiggles in excitement. "Tanner is outside with a limo!"

Some people gasp and others cheer. The waitress comes back with our checks and hurries away when Sonny bumps into her.

"Sorry, ma'am," he mumbles at the woman maybe a year older than us, if any.

It will be interesting to watch him dance with Carolina at the prom. She's very dainty and light on her feet. He's a football player who walks like Shrek.

Jonah stares at Carolina from across the table. They're good friends, but I think he wants more. Too bad they both brought different dates.

"Kids, y'all ready?" Tanner's voice calls from the door.

He's standing by Paul, who is dressed like the limo driver from *Home Alone 2*. Quite the change from his usual jeans and big belt buckle.

"What's Paul doing here?" Kristie asks with a tense jaw.

She's been scared of Paul's General Store her entire life. It's rumored he keeps coffins in the back. Of course, the sign above the door, "From a Cradle to a Coffin," only adds to that theory.

Tanner slaps him on the shoulder. "It's his limo."

"You kids are in luck. I traded my hearse for this beauty last week."

Kristie's face matches the white napkin on her chest. I watch a lump trickle down her throat.

Carolina winces. I think she assumed Tanner rented a limo from a legit rental place like most people.

"Y'all ready?" Tanner smiles as if the hearse comment is normal. I suppose it is for Paul.

As if on cue, the waitress comes back to collect cards and cash. Kristie takes her to-go box, while the rest of us focus on Tanner and Paul.

"We'll be out in a minute," Nate answers.

Tanner nods, smiling so widely, his dimples pop. He turns, pulling Paul out the door with him.

We sit in awkward silence as we wait on the waitress to return our cards and change. Nobody really knows what to do with Paul.

He's super kind and friendly. His store, though strange, is kind of a staple in our town. It's been there, like, forever.

Then again, he's weird. His store is weird, he dresses like a flashy cowboy, and he's always showing up at places for free food—like my cousin's eighth birthday party. He's not family or even really a friend of our family. He just came to the party, grabbed cake and ice cream, then left. At least he brought a gift.

Wait . . . I think he brought the puppet doll that gave her nightmares. I shudder at the memory.

"You cold?" Nate rubs my shoulders.

"I'm fine."

"Here." He pulls his jacket from his chair and wraps it around me.

It engulfs me like a blanket out of the dryer. His clean aftershave scent tickles my nose. I need to bottle his scent before we all go to college.

The waitress returns and everyone prepares to leave. I stand slowly, tugging the jacket more securely over my shoulders. Nate puts his hand on my back and leads me behind our friends.

I soak in everything—his smell, the way his big hand stretches across my back, the laughter of our friends, the glitter and glam of us wearing suits and gowns instead of jeans and sweatshirts. If I could bottle this moment, I would. I could make a shadow box of it and carry it with me to college, and beyond.

Regardless of where we all end up, nothing will be the same ever again.

I swallow and try to live in the moment. Paul helps burst my sentimental bubble by jumping in front of Kristie.

"I'll keep that up front for safety." He jerks the to-go box from her hand.

Her jaw drops and she blinks. Bless her heart. She already looks terrified to get in the limo.

Tanner swings the back door open and fans his hand. "Ladies and gents, your carriage awaits."

Kristie hangs back as everyone else files in. I step beside her. "It'll be fine. We're all going in."

She takes a deep breath, then enters with me. Tanner shuts the door behind us.

I scan the inside. It's like we entered a time warp back to the seventies. A disco ball hangs from the center of the roof, and the red seats are a vinyl material.

"Who stole Austin Powers' shag wagon?" Sonny laughs.

Carolina narrows her eyes at him. "It was free."

He kicks his big feet up on the seat across, bumping them into Kristie. She flinches. Poor thing is on edge.

The window separating the front rolls down, and Tanner sticks his head through it. "Next stop, prom?"

Everyone nods. Nobody wants to go on a rogue road trip with Tanner and Paul, especially in this thing.

"It will be hard topping this for our senior prom," Jonah jokes with Carolina.

I half smile. Last year, I assumed my senior prom would be carefree, but it isn't. As a junior, I didn't have a care in the world beyond high school. Now it's hard to enjoy the moment, knowing I've got actual adult decisions to make.

Like am I going to UA as I've always planned, or will I follow Nate to MSU? Yes, I know following a guy is never a good idea. But I love him, and he will be so busy with baseball.

Jonah does something stupid, and everyone laughs. The way his date is blushing, I hate that I missed it.

That's enough. I need to be in the moment and enjoy my senior prom. So far I've managed to not spill anything on my red dress, and thanks to Adrianne, my hair and makeup are flawless.

I smile at Nate and he gives me a gentle kiss on the cheek.

No matter what the next few months hold, tonight can be fun and carefree.

Nate

Tinsel slaps me in the face when we enter the gym. I duck and lead Brooke across the threshold. She's wearing tall shoes and tall hair, and she cleared the entrance fine.

I smile at the memory of the time I figured out we're eye to eye when she stands one bleacher up from me. From then on, that's how I kissed her after every football game. Even the last two years, when I stopped football to play year-round baseball. After the cheerleaders left the field, she'd meet me in the bleachers to carry on the tradition.

The last football game was bittersweet, but not nearly as much as the last baseball game. At least for me, the game will continue. The bigger question is where?

I've gotten an offer from Mississippi State, but some scout got my number and promised he'd call.

I sigh. No use getting my hopes up over a dangling carrot. Most likely I'll go to college.

Brooke's eyes light up at the dance floor. I've never been much of a dancer. Now that I think of it, the only times I've danced is with her. Not that I'm complaining.

I'm beyond lucky to call her my girlfriend. She's smart, sweet, and beautiful. And her family reminds me of what you see in movies. The kind where everyone is happy and working together, not some slapstick comedy with rednecks. That would be my story.

Dad left when I was a toddler, so I was raised by a single mom who put me in baseball to keep me busy between school and her getting off work. I love my mom and my life, but it's a far cry from Brooke growing up on a freaking apple farm her great-grandparents started.

My phone buzzes in my pocket. I click the side to silence it and fall under Brooke's spell as she wraps her little arms around me and gently strokes the back of my neck. The DJ plays that old song "Time After Time," and my mind flashes to all our memories.

We started kindergarten together, but didn't start dating until beginning of sophomore year. That was about the time I considered anything other than baseball, which included how pretty some of the girls looked.

Brooke was never the fanciest or flashiest, but she's always been the most beautiful to me.

The kind of girl who looks just as good with a ponytail and no makeup as she does tonight with her big hair and red lipstick. Once I started noticing her more, I learned she's also kind and smart and fun. That's all it took for me to decide I needed to ask her to the homecoming dance.

We've been together ever since.

I dip my head closer to her, and she smiles up at me. Her brown eyes twinkle in the crazy colored lighting. The gym has a retro thing going on. Maybe that's why they're playing some old songs, and possibly why we rode in a limo that probably looked the same when our parents went to prom.

"Remember the first time we danced together?" Brooke's smile stretches across her face.

"I do. I was actually just thinking of that."

"Were you?" Her smile has a hint of mischief, and my toes curl.

"It was in here after homecoming."

"Yep." She laughs.

"I knew that night that you liked me a lot."

"Oh, did you?"

"Yes, because I stunk horribly and you still wrapped your arms around me and danced close."

She blushes. "Am I that easy to read?"

I shrug. "For me, maybe."

"Well, we were still in uniform, but at least you took your pads off."

"At least we won after two overtimes."

She sighs. "Yeah, why we played Wisteria on Homecoming that year is still a mystery."

I laugh. "They'd have done better with me off the team."

"Stop it." She swats my chest playfully. "You were a good backup quarterback."

"Meh." I snarl. "Football's more fun to watch. Baseball's more fun to play."

"To each his own. Football is more fun to cheer for."

I chuckle. "Since there's so many baseball cheer squads."

"If there were, I'd gladly join to cheer for you." She touches my nose and wrinkles hers at the same time.

It's those cheesy yet adorable qualities that will make her the perfect elementary teacher one day.

"You cheer me on already, and you're the only cheerleader I need."

My phone buzzes again and I reach to silence it. The song ends and a fast song comes on. That Maroon 5 one about "Sugar."

Everyone cheers and starts dancing in ways I don't know how. My phone buzzes again, and this time I reach for it. Brooke is already dancing with Kristie and her date beside her. I raise my phone, and Brooke nods.

Great excuse to not embarrass my clumsy self.

I freeze when I see the name on the screen.

Wally Guy . . . the scout who came to two of my games.

Even with shaky hands, I somehow manage to answer it. "Hello?" I hurry off the dance floor at the sound of Wally's voice.

He's loud, but the people screaming and laughing are louder.

"Are you there, Nate?"

I jog to the edge of the gym and stop in the hallway. "Yeah, I'm here."

Two people peek from around a locker. Sonny is sharing one of those electric cigarettes with a girl named Aniston. He runs away when he sees me. She winks at me. I roll my eyes and keep walking.

"I know you've been talking to MSU, but have you given any thought to going pro?"

Have I? Only every waking moment since I was about seven.

Once the shock wears off, I pinch myself.

"Nate?"

"Sir, uh, yes, sir." I clear my throat, not liking how eager I sound.

I've secretly practiced a conversation like this so I could play it cool. But the real deal isn't as easy as staring in the bathroom mirror.

"I wanted to check before you start any college classes. If you don't go in the draft now, then you'll have to wait three more years."

I swallow. Three years.

A lot could happen in three years. I could be almost done with college and have collegiate baseball experience.

Or I could go pro, help Mom with money, and go back to school anytime. Besides, I'm at the peak of my physical ability. My brain has more time than my arm.

"I'd be a fool to waste an opportunity like that."

"I knew you were a sharp young man."

I smile as Wally briefly describes some of the process and when I would need to decide.

"Can I talk to my mom about it?"

"Of course, son. I'd be worried if you didn't."

"Okay." I take a deep breath, then exhale.

"We'll talk soon. Enjoy your weekend."

"Yes, sir, you too."

I slide my phone in my pocket and rake my hand through my hair. My life could change drastically in the next few months.

"Nate!"

I turn to Carolina yelling my name from the gym door. She motions for me to come back.

I jog toward her, silently worried something happened to Brooke. No matter what goes on in life, my biggest fears are something happening to Brooke or my mom.

Carolina grabs my arm and jerks me through the tinsel. For someone small, she has quite a grip. "Everyone is hunting you."

My eyes find Brooke in the front center of the dance floor with a crown on her head. One of the junior cheerleaders stands beside her with a more goofy-looking crown.

"And there's our prom king," Kevin says over a microphone.

I don't see him, but I know his voice. He's class president, does debate stuff, and emcees a lot of things at the school. He's pretty much the Ryan Seacrest of Apple Cart County High.

People clap, but it's muffled behind my thoughts of Brooke and the phone call with Wally. I march toward her, and Emma slaps the crown on my head. She smiles at us, then moves back.

"Time for the king and queen to have their dance," Kevin announces.

I fumble with the stupid circle shoved on my head, then take Brooke in my arms. *Try and pretend nobody is watching us.* I'm used to people staring at me while I pitch, but this is different. I'm wearing a monkey suit and a plastic crown, and we're dancing.

Brooke smiles. "I was beginning to wonder if you'd stood me up."

"I had to find a quiet place to talk."

Her face falls. "Is everything okay?"

"Yeah." I shake my head. "Actually, it's great."

One side of her mouth lifts.

"That was Wally."

"Wally?"

"Yeah, the recruiter guy who came to watch me a few times."

"Oh." Her eyes widen. "He called you?"

"Yeah."

"What for?"

I take a deep breath and look her in the eye. I can't wait for her reaction.

"He wants to put me in the draft."

Her forehead wrinkles. "Wait, draft? As in to play professional baseball?"

"Well, it isn't to be in the military." I laugh. "Of course for baseball. Isn't that great?"

She looks away and frowns. Not the reaction I was expecting, and certainly not the one I was hoping for.

"Brooke? Isn't that great?"

Her eyes cut back to me, a little glossy. *Please don't cry!*

"Where will you go?"

I lift and lower my shoulder. "Dunno yet. Could be anywhere, really. Most likely I'll have to start out in the minors, and there are a lot of those teams around."

She gives me a forced smile. I'd rather her frown again, since I know when she's faking. I close my eyes for a second to refocus. The "Thinking Out Loud" song is playing.

If I think out loud right now, I might break Brooke. Instead, I pull her closer and dance like we have plenty of times before.

This is the only kind of dancing I like. The only kind I do well. Holding her tightly and moving super slow like this moment will go on forever.

CHAPTER 2

Brooke

Don't cry, don't cry, don't cry.

There are so many reasons I don't need to cry. I don't want to mess up my makeup before prom king and queen pictures, I don't want to look weak, and most of all, don't want Nate to know I'm worried.

He was supposed to play college baseball. Then after college, we could get married and go wherever he wanted. I'm going to be a teacher. Schools are everywhere.

So are baseball teams.

But so are cleat chasers.

Insecurities overwhelm me and my eyes moisten. I squeeze them tightly to try and hold back the tears. I can't ruin Nate's dream. I refuse to be selfish and ask him to wait on me.

But all I can think about is him moving across the country and spending time with some other girl, then forgetting about me.

The song starts to end, and I open my eyes. Becki is walking toward us with a camera. My body tenses. She's going to want our photo for the yearbook.

I can't let her do that until I check my eyes.

"What's wrong?" Nate whispers against my ear.

I'm sure he sensed the tension, as my arms are now like tree branches propped against his shoulders.

"I've got to go to the restroom for a minute."

I slide away from him and hold my dress so I can hurry toward the hallway without tripping.

I'm five foot three on a good posture day, and Nate is every bit of six foot two. Anytime we plan on dancing together, I wear super-tall shoes.

The few people not caught up in their own dates or drama turn their heads as I dart through the crowd. I mutter "excuse me" and brush past couples and groups dancing and talking.

When I exit the gym, I see dots as my eyes adjust to the full lighting. My heels click, echoing down the hallway.

I open the bathroom door to Aniston. "Is prom over?"

"No." I squeeze around her and go to the mirror.

"Did you win queen?"

"Yes."

She laughs and leaves.

I try and not take it personally. She's a rebel and doesn't like anything at school. I make it a point to be nice to her when I see her, since she's also a bit of a loner.

My eye makeup is still intact. Adrianne said the mascara she used would withstand a storm. Maybe a storm includes ugly crying, which I'm desperately trying to prevent.

I lift a shaky hand to blot a stray tear. The door opens again, and I flinch. "Nate! You can't be in here."

"Then you need to come out, because I want to check on you."

I lean against the sink and sigh. "I'm fine."

"Are you sick?"

I shake my head.

"Then do you want to come back to the gym?"

I shrug, then glance around. "We really need to get out of here. If someone sees you in here—"

"What? They'll expel us? Baseball season is over, and we graduate in a month. There's not much they can do to me now."

"They could tell the college."

He grins. "I'm not going to college now, remember?"

My stomach knots and I fold my arms across it. I rush past him and shove the door open with my shoulder.

"Brooke!" I've made it maybe a few feet when he calls me. I'm surprised he didn't stop me in the bathroom.

"Brooke, wait." His voice is close, but I keep clicking my heels. I make it outside to the parking lot before his large hand catches my arm. "Brooke, what's wrong? Please tell me."

I face him, no longer able to fight off tears. The floodgates open when I stare into his brown puppy-dog eyes. "I don't want you to go."

"Go where? Back to the prom?"

"No." I laugh, but it comes out strained.

"What do you mean?"

I throw my hands up. "I don't want to ruin your life, but I don't want to lose you, either."

His jaw drops, along with my tears.

So many emotions swirl through my body. I'm upset, embarrassed, scared. My skin is flush, but I have shivers. I've never felt so much at once, and it scares me.

Nate runs his hands up and down my bare arms. My nerves flare as his calloused fingers brush my skin. "Don't ever say you'll lose me. You can't lose me."

I blink, sending a stream of tears down my cheeks. Nate moves one of his hands to wipe my face. I stare at him and try to make sense of everything. "I can't expect you to wait for me while you're playing ball."

"Wait for you?"

I nod. "Yeah, while I'm in college. If you're not in college, then we'll be on different timelines."

He laughs. "What are you talking about? We're the same age. I'll be playing ball no matter what. Except instead of ball paying for school, I'll be getting paid to play."

I bite my bottom lip to keep from crying. It doesn't work.

Nate loves me. I know he does. But if he's halfway across the country on a ball team, I can't expect him to stay with me.

"This way I can help my mom financially. I'll play while I'm still young and fresh. Then I can go to college later if I want."

I swallow. He makes a lot of sense. Playing pro ball was always his dream, and this is too good to pass up.

Too bad my dream was for his dream to happen on a different timeline.

Wow. I sound like a selfish brat.

Nate smiles, and I blink back a lingering tear. I have to let him do this. His mom raised him alone, and he wants to make sure she's set for the future. And it does make sense to play pro if he can right away, while he's in optimal shape.

"I . . ." My mouth won't work.

Nate leans his head closer to mine and kisses me.

Slowly, my mouth comes alive as I kiss him back. It's a wonderful kiss—until my head gets in the way.

Not in the way of bumping against his, but in the way of my mind dwelling on all the "ifs" for our future. Then my head literally gets in the way as I shake it and pull back.

"What?"

A horn honks to the tune of "Dixie."

Nate and I both turn to the old limo peeling through the parking lot. It stops a few feet from us, and Tanner hops out the passenger side.

"Hey, can one of you get Carolina? Her curfew's coming up."

"I will." I turn and rush toward the entrance.

I glance back before opening the door. Tanner is talking to Nate. Good. He has bought me time to think before having the dreaded conversation with my boyfriend.

Carolina is sitting in the bleachers with Jonah and his date.

"Hey, Tanner is here for you."

She perks up and grabs my hand. We rush toward the gym exit together.

"Thank you," she says once we're outside the prom area. "I texted him to pick me up. One of my friends saw Sonny smoking with Aniston. I don't want him to leave with me."

"Understood." I wrap an arm around her shoulder.

Nate opens his mouth to say something when we get to the limo, but I speak first. "I'm going to ride with Carolina. I'll see you later?"

His face wrinkles with confusion. I lean forward and kiss him on the cheek.

With a somewhat satisfied expression on his face, he nods. I climb in the back with Carolina, and Tanner slams the door behind us.

Before I can even sit down properly, Paul takes off and Carolina starts spilling the details of her night. "Prom wasn't anything like I'd thought it would be."

Amen, sister!

Nate

What just happened?

Twenty minutes ago, I'm dancing with my girlfriend to one of our favorite songs. Now I'm standing in the parking lot as she rides away in a hunk-of-junk limo with the Nash siblings and Paul.

What the crap?

Even worse, my truck is still down the interstate at Applebee's.

I wipe a hand down my face and turn toward the school. If I go back in, there will be questions.

Becki will want our photo, and that will lead to everyone asking where Brooke went.

Ah, screw it. I've got to find out what's wrong with Brooke.

I sneak toward the gym door and peek inside. Jonah and his date are near the exit, talking.

"Jonah," I whisper.

He turns to me and his eyebrows pull together. "What are you doing?"

I reach in the door and jerk him outside. He stumbles a little, then straightens his lanky frame.

"Sorry, man. I need to get to my truck."

"Well, I'm about to leave. Sydney wants to stay longer, and I'm not really into this. Besides, I think Carolina needs me."

"Cool." I frown. "Wait, y'all rode in the limo with us."

"Yeah, but Tanner's truck is parked here, so I can drive it."

"Thanks, man."

"Let me tell Sydney real quick. I'll meet you at Tanner's truck."

I nod and return to the parking lot. About the time I figure out the truck is locked, Jonah walks toward me. "Do you have the keys?" I ask.

"He said they're in it when I texted him."

"Well, he locked the stupid truck."

Jonah sighs. "Doesn't surprise me."

"What are we going to do?"

Without saying a word, Jonah climbs in the bed of the truck. He pulls a pocket knife from his pants pocket and opens the blade. Then he meticulously does something with the sealing of the back window until it opens.

I watch in awe as he slinks his long, slim body through the small back opening and unlocks the cab.

I'm still in shock when he rolls down the window and sticks his head out. "Are you coming?"

I grin and rush to the passenger side.

On the way to Applebee's, I stay quiet except for a few comments here and there. Jonah talks plenty for the both of us about Carolina and how Sonny's not good enough for her.

I totally agree, but I think Jonah is a little jealous.

I don't dare tell him that though, as it's none of my business and the two need to sort it out themselves.

Applebee's is closed and the only remnants of life are our vehicles and the dessert special lit up on a sign.

"Thanks again, man, I owe you one," I say.

"No problem. Congrats on king."

I look up and frown at the cheesy crown I forgot I was still wearing. I take it off and groan.

Jonah chuckles. "You forgot all about that thing, didn't you?"

I twirl it on my hand. "Yep. Shocking since it's so beautiful."

He laughs harder. "Well, go see your queen."

"You too."

Jonah narrows his eyes as if trying to figure out if I mean Carolina. Before I get into anything that isn't my business, I jump out of Tanner's truck and get in mine.

I toss the silly crown in the passenger seat and drive as fast as safely possible toward the apple orchard.

Brooke's pretty face drenched in tears haunts my mind as

I pass our town, then houses and fields, before seeing rows of apple trees.

Her house is lit up from the drive, but I slow down to not disturb her family. The porch light is on, and I see shadows from the rocking chair.

I park out front and hurry up the porch.

"Tanner?" My heartbeat increases when I see Tanner sitting beside Brooke. She's wearing pajamas and slippers.

He jumps up and fear flashes across his face. "I'm just waiting for Paul to come out. He's talking to Brooke's parents."

Brooke shrugs. "I changed for bed, and they were still here."

Sure enough, a second later, Paul comes out the door with a personal-size apple pie. The kind Brooke's family sells at the orchard store. "Ready?" he asks.

"Been ready. I'm not paying you extra for socializing." Tanner groans.

Paul laughs and adjusts his weird little driver's hat. Then he struts down the porch with Tanner behind him.

"Well, that was strange." I take off my jacket and lay it across the back of the swing, then sit beside Brooke.

She smiles at me sadly. I wrap my arm around her shoulder. "Brooke, dumpling, what's wrong?"

Her lips twitch, and I almost make her smile. I nicknamed her "dumpling" as a joke, then it stuck. She made me apple dumplings on the anniversary of our first year dating. I kidded that she was my favorite dumpling.

"I can't mess up your life."

"What?"

She inhales, then exhales deeply. I watch her chest rise and fall and notice the red splotches on her neck. They're almost the same color as her bright pink pajamas.

"I thought you would go play at State. I was considering going there but would probably stick with UA. Either way, we could be close. Then we would both graduate, and I could follow you to wherever you played professionally."

I sigh and run my hand over my hair. Guilt floods my insides. I hadn't considered that this would bother her so much.

"Brooke, there's a chance I might not get drafted in college. This could be my only shot at pro ball. You know I don't have a lot financially. I don't want my mom to work so hard for little pay her whole life when I can help."

"I know." She rests her small hand on my leg.

"No matter where we are, we will always be together."

She turns away from me and stares into the dark. I hook a finger under her chin and gently turn her face toward me. "Hey, don't worry about me ever not being with you."

A tear falls down her cheek. She wipes it and sniffles. "I will not be one of those women who holds you back."

"You're not holding me back."

She sniffles again. I move my hand to wipe away another tear, then rest it on her knee.

"Not now, but what if you go across the country? Playing for MSU, I knew you'd be traveling a lot. But if you're traveling and located in a faraway place, we'll never see each other. I can't expect us to stay together like that."

"Yes we will." My stomach pits at those words leaving her mouth. I don't want her to doubt us, ever. "You can come to games or come visit me when you're not in school."

"But it's college. That's harder than high school. I'll be studying and have exams."

I laugh. "You're the smartest person I know. Heck, you got me through most of math."

She laughs through her tears.

"Look, why don't we not worry about this now. Nothing's been decided. I could end up someplace local or no place at all and go to college. We don't know anything yet. You're the only person I've told so far. I don't even want to tell Mom until I'm sure this might pan out."

Finally, I get her to smile. I stand and pull her to her feet. "I think you owe me a dance."

She smiles wider and wipes her wet cheeks. I pull my phone from my pocket and find the same Ed Sheeran song they played during our king and queen dance. Since Paul tipped me off that her family isn't asleep, I turn up the volume.

Without her heels, Brooke's head lands square at my chest. As much as I love staring at her beautiful face, I adore having her breathe against my heartbeats. I hug her closer and sway across the wooden porch.

The apple tree leaves rustle in the breeze and her sweet scent travels toward my nose. I run my hand up and down the back of her satin pajama shirt and commit this moment to memory.

If this draft thing works out, I don't know how many more chances I'll get to dance with her on this porch.

CHAPTER 3

Brooke

"Ahh!" A balloon pops in my face and I fall on my butt.

The people actually trying to read in the library give me a dirty look.

"Sorry." I wince.

I twist the shriveled balloon in the arch to hide it and take my time adjusting the last few. After a few squeaky minutes and more stares from the occupants nearby, I stand back and admire my work.

Not bad. I smile to myself and let out a sigh.

I want everything to be nice and memorable for Nate's signing day.

The last few weeks have been a whirlwind. He joined the draft and got picked up by the Braves. No, not *the* Braves. A minor league team called the Gwinnett Braves that's associated with the MLB team.

The good news is he will be stationed in Georgia, so still

not too far. The bad news is we will both be so busy, I'm not sure how much we will see one another.

I turned in my final paperwork to Bama last week, confirming that I'd start in August.

"Hello, sweet Brooke," Nate's mama calls from the doorway in her soothing voice.

"Hey, Ms. Anne."

She shifts the box she's carrying to one hip and gives me a side hug.

"Let me help you." I clear a place on a nearby table for her to set the box.

We unload Dollar General bags full of cups, plates, forks, and napkins. All are red and navy for the Braves.

"That looks nice." Her eyes trail the balloon arch that took me way longer than the packaging suggested.

"Thanks."

"My friend Carla made these. Aren't they cute?" She pulls a rectangular container from the bottom of the cardboard box and opens it. It's an assortment of cookies in the shapes of tomahawks and the letters GB.

"Wow, those look great."

"Don't they? I told Carla she should do this stuff more often."

Anne pulls a plastic platter from the box and wipes it down. I watch as she meticulously arranges the cookies on the plate.

She's a pretty woman, but always looks tired. She works full time at the hospital office, and fills in for doctors too. When she's not working, she's going to Nate's games or washing his uniforms. No wonder he wants to help her.

Something heavy plops on my shoulder. I turn to Nate with one arm draped around me and one around his mother.

"Hey, son." She hugs him.

"Looks great in here." He smiles at her, then me. "I've never seen a library look so good."

A guy of similar stature to Nate walks in with an older balding guy. Nate introduces them as the pitching coach for the Gwinnett team and Wally.

I put on my Southern belle sweetness while I'm introduced. So does Anne. When they start talking ball jargon, I zone out. Anne smiles at me and busies herself with stacking napkins. She probably feels the same way.

Coach Randy enters with the vice principal and several senior baseball players. A few more teachers and friends of Nate's trickle in and sit in the rows of chairs lined in front of the table. Nate and his mom sit at the head table under my balloon monster, between Coach Randy and the pitching coach.

I stand to the side and search for a good place to take photos. Principal Fowler starts to talk, then pauses when Nate walks away. He grabs an empty chair from the corner of the library, then sets it on the other side of him.

I don't realize what's going on until he takes my hand and leads me behind the head table. I sit between him and Coach, my face flush with embarrassment.

I've been in front of crowds plenty, but I've never been comfortable being put on the spot. I slide the chair closer to the table, and Nate puts his hand on my knee. He grins at me and whispers, "I wanted you with me."

My heart flips. I look at everyone in front of us. Teachers, students, friends.

There's a good chance this group will never be in the same place again after graduation. Everyone has a plan, whether college, work, and now the minor leagues.

Applause fills the room, and I turn to Nate scribbling his name on a piece of paper. He slides it to the Braves coach and they shake hands.

Becki snaps a picture, then a larger camera almost blinds me. It's a guy I recognize from the local newspaper.

Fowler stands and adjusts his glasses. "Ms. Miller has

refreshments if anyone wants to stay and congratulate Nate. Just make sure you don't need to get to class."

Several of our friends frown, and I notice at least two eye rolls. It's hard to take going to class seriously when our grades are submitted and we're two weeks from graduating.

Both coaches and Wally are grouped together talking, with Nate nearby. People come up to congratulate him on their way to get refreshments. I stand to the side awkwardly before helping Anne put ice in cups.

It's hard to know my place in all this, or if I even have a place at all. I don't want to cling to Nate and keep him from his goals and duties, but I also want to be alongside him to support him.

After all the cups are filled and everyone either grabs a drink or leaves the library, I sit down with some friends.

"I can't believe Fowler wanted us to go back to class," Kristie moans.

"We've all gotten into college and sent transcripts. I just come every day to hang out with y'all." Mark shoves a cookie in his mouth.

"Well, unlike you lucky people, I'm still a junior." Stephen stands and sighs. "If I don't get back to geometry, Mrs. Martin will make me take the final I was barely exempted from." He downs the rest of his drink and waves to Nate on the way out.

Kristie smiles at Nate, then hugs me. "You must be so excited for him. Nobody from our school has made it past college ball."

"I am." I hug her back.

"See ya later." She pats my back, then leaves.

I watch Nate chatting with everyone. He hasn't smiled this big in a long time. I'm happy for him, and hope it's everything he's ever dreamed about.

Now I need to figure out the best way I can help with that.

Nate

Brooke laughs as the chef lights a stack of onion slices and they smoke like a tiny volcano.

I've never even tried sushi, but she loves this place. I come for two reasons—Brooke and the fried rice.

The guy slings metal spatulas like a cowboy does his gun in a western. Except I've never seen a cowboy toss an egg onto his hat, then catch it on his gun.

Seeing Brooke happy and relaxed is what I needed to officially make this the perfect day. She was extra quiet earlier at my signing. I hope it's because she'd never been at something like that, and not because she wished I wasn't signing.

"Yo!" The guy bounces a piece of chicken on the spatula and nods at me.

I'm not refined enough for sushi, but this I can handle. I open my mouth wide and use my highly developed hand-eye coordination as he bats the chicken with the spatula. It lands on my tongue like I'm a golden retriever.

The older couple sitting across the grill from us claps and cheers. Brooke laughs and pats my leg. "Good job."

"That's my favorite part of coming here."

"Really?" She wrinkles her cute little nose.

"I like the rice too." I reach under the table and hold her hand. "I know you love it here. You wanted to come for prom, didn't you?"

"Yeah, but I also wanted to go with our friends."

"And their fancy is like Applebee's."

Brooke giggles. "That should be a slogan."

"If I ever get important enough to endorse Applebee's, I'll suggest that." I wink.

Her eyes twitch and cloud over slightly.

"You okay?"

"Yeah." She shakes her head. "Must be the smoke from this grill."

"Yo!" The cook commands everyone's attention again before scooping spatulas full of rice on everyone's plate.

I polish off my soup, then Brooke's, while the rice cools. I always trade my salad for her soup.

We eat quietly while he cooks vegetables, then meat. Someone brings Brooke's big plate of sushi. I squirm when she picks up a piece with chopsticks.

"You think this is gross, don't you?" She smirks.

I shrug. "Meat should be grilled or fried, not rolled in rice."

She laughs and takes a big bite of the roll. I take my fork and analyze the remains of what she bit into.

"What's even in this?" I fork a piece of something green and rake it onto her plate.

"That's a cucumber."

"Then what about this slimy stuff?" I stab at something else green.

Brooke laughs. "That's avocado."

I shake my head.

She picks apart the rest with a chopstick. "This is shrimp, crab, rice." She smiles at me. "See? Nothing weird or foreign, and the meat is cooked."

"I'll stick to my plate." I pick up my fork and stab a piece of steak.

We continue eating and joking with each other. The older couple across from us provides some entertainment too. I don't think they've ever been here. The man looks as clueless as I am about sushi.

He also looks amazed when I polish off all my food and finish what's left of Brooke's. Except for the sushi, of course.

I try not to wince when I see our bill. Applebee's is more my speed too. But I try to take Brooke someplace nice on occasion.

She goes nice places with her family all the time, and they take me when I'm available. Never has she complained about us eating fast food or renting movies instead of going to the theater. That makes me want to treat her even more.

Most girls of her status would turn their nose up at some of our dates. Brooke isn't like that. She would go and do anything as long as we're together, and that's one of the many things I love about her.

I thumb out enough twenties to cover the bill and leave a tip. Good thing I'm giving a few pitching lessons next week. I'm about out of gas money.

The waitress collects our pay and grins at my empty plate. She brought the older couple a to-go box, but I declined when she offered one to Brooke.

"He told you he'd eat the rest," Brooke laughs.

"And he did." She scans the table, smiling. "I'll be right back."

"I don't need change."

"Oh thanks." She smiles wider. "Y'all have a good evening."

I stand and put my hand on Brooke's back when she gets up. Better to leave now before the giddy waitress finds out I only left her two bucks. Not out of greed, but out of necessity.

We leave the smoke and sizzles behind and step into downtown Tuscaloosa.

"How cute. This must've just opened." Brooke points to an older building across the street.

"Looks like a coffee shop. Want some?"

She nods enthusiastically.

I take her hand and wait for the okay to cross the street.

The last thing I need is to spend money on overpriced coffee, but I have enough gas to get us home. Besides, we have a lot to celebrate. I'm going to play minor league ball, and Brooke's about to start college. Oh, and we graduate in a week.

Funny how I keep forgetting about that.

We jog across the street and stop in front of metal letters that spell out "The Coffee Loft." For me, the scent of coffee is way better than the taste. I usually let Brooke order for me and tell her I want it to taste more like milk.

A long list of flavor options is written across a chalkboard behind the counter. With tons of chocolate, vanilla, and caramel choices, I get the courage to order myself.

They also have some cookies and pastries under a glass case, but I'm too full for that. Brooke's rice pushed me over the edge.

She orders her usual vanilla cappuccino, and I go for chocolate-chip flavored.

"Would you like fries with that?" the hippie-looking cashier asks.

Brooke and I exchange a confused look. There's a lot of treats on the menu, but I didn't notice fries.

"My bad." After a loud, goofy laugh, he adds, "I was at McDonald's before this place opened. Kind of ironic since I make drinks all the time here and their milkshake machine never worked."

Brooke chokes a little trying to hide a laugh. I clear my throat to do the same as I pay for our drinks.

We step to the side, and I scan the room while we wait on our order. It's one of those old buildings with a tall ceiling that shows the pipes. The walls are brick, and the tables and chairs don't all match.

We collect our drinks and sit in the corner at a small table with two chairs. Brooke blows into the small opening of her lid. That always makes me laugh, since I doubt it helps.

I take a small sip of mine. "This is good."

Brooke stops blowing and sips hers cautiously. "Mine too."

"This isn't far from campus. You could come here when you need some caffeine."

She takes another drink, then sighs.

I reach across the table for her hand. "You'll be awesome in college. You're so smart and friendly."

One side of her mouth lifts into an almost smile. "It's just odd to think we won't be in high school anymore after next week, or even in Apple Cart after the summer."

I squeeze my paper cup and swallow a big gulp of chocolate coffee. I've been putting off something long enough.

"I leave for Atlanta in a month."

She lowers her cup from her mouth and rubs her lips together. Her eyes move from my eyes to my lips and back as if she's processing what I just said. "As in June?"

I nod.

Her mouth opens into a small O shape.

"I know you aren't moving until August, but they need me there to practice." I rest my hand on hers. "You can come visit me, and I can visit you when I get a chance."

She smiles sadly and stares at me for a long minute. I rub the back of her hand with my thumb.

At last, she speaks. "We have a full month together."

"And it will be the best month of our lives."

"So far." Brooke's eyes soften.

I set my cup on the table and wrap my other hand around hers. "Good point. We have the rest of our lives to spend together."

I study her face and commit every feature to memory, from her big brown eyes to her small pink lips. Neither of us say it, but we don't have to.

This next month will be the most time we have together for a long time.

CHAPTER 4

Nate

The one kid with a Z name shakes hands with the principal and takes his diploma. A weird mixture of relief and nostalgia covers me.

Like it or not, I'm now an official adult.

"May I present to you the Apple Cart County High School class of 2015," Principal Fowler announces.

Applause fills the stadium, and I join my classmates in tossing my hat. It snows red squares as the hats fall around us. Everyone scatters to find their hats while family and friends leave the bleachers.

I shuffle down our row to Brooke. We're only a few seats apart, since both our last names start with M.

She wraps her arms around my waist and squeezes me tightly. "We did it."

"We did." I kiss the top of her head.

People bump into my back as they hurry out of their own seats. Brooke and I walk toward the open area just in time for her cousin to find us. Erica hugs us both and mumbles something excitedly.

We hug her back and share an amused look over her head. She graduated last year and lobbied for everyone to go to Auburn with her. Neither of us did, but several Apple Cart kids are already there or plan to go. Like Tanner and Carolina.

I wave to my mom. Brooke's parents are beside her, and they notice us at the same time. Several friends come by and congratulate us before our parents make it to the field.

My buddy Aaron grabs my shoulder and talks close. "Y'all coming to the field later?"

"Maybe. I gotta let Mom take photos and stuff."

He smirks. "Yeah, I gotta get that over with too."

The field is code for the field down the road from Brooke's orchard. It's owned by the county and used for a golf course, but they also put cattle on it. Weird, but it somehow works.

They have cattle now, so nobody should be complaining about people on the grass. When it's not golf season, we can get away with building a fire near the edge of the woods. Some of us guys have camped there a few times too.

Mom finds us and hugs us almost as aggressively as Erica. Possibly the same if you account for their age difference.

"Let me get some photos," she says before anything else.

I sigh and try not to show my annoyance too much. I don't care for a bunch of photos. However, I play nice for the parents. Who knows when this group of friends will be together again for photos—if ever.

Brooke's grandpa shuffles toward us and motions her grandma our way. "Come on, Edna. Let's get a photo first so we can sit down again."

I bite my tongue to keep from laughing. Old people can get away with saying anything.

The next half hour is spent smiling and hugging and trying not to tangle my long limbs in the robe thing they made us wear.

As people start to spread apart, the microphone squeals. I stick my finger in my ear and give it a good shake. Mrs. Mary is at the podium, pulling the mic down since Fowler's got quite a few inches on her. "Everyone's welcome at the diner for refreshments," she yells.

I shake both ears this time. People smile and applaud, almost as much as for our graduation. It will be interesting to see how we all fit in the tiny restaurant.

"Should we go?" Brooke asks.

"I'll leave that up to you."

I know our time together is limited, as well as my time in this town. As usual, I defer to whatever she wants.

She shrugs. "Should be fun."

"I want to take this off first." I tug at the neck of my robe.

Brooke laughs.

"After a few more pictures," Mom says. She lifts her camera and motions for us to scoot together. Brooke is under one of my arms and one of my buddies leans on the other shoulder. I hear more people joining the photo.

Mom takes several before we're allowed to split. I unzip the robe and jerk it off. She takes it and folds it like it's a precious keepsake. Maybe it is to her. I hand her my hat, and Brooke gives her graduation suit to her mom. Now we're left standing in new church clothes.

"Oh, you two look so nice. One more photo."

Brooke laughs and pulls me beside her to appease my mom. As much as I hate taking photos, having her beside me makes it worth it.

Mom snaps several pictures before she's satisfied. Then she smiles and turns the camera for Brooke's mom to see.

"We have great-looking kids," Mrs. Margaret comments.

"We sure do," Mom agrees. She sniffles a little.

Maybe she won't cry. I know her breakdown is coming, but I'm not ready for it tonight.

"Are y'all fine if we head to Mary's Diner?" I ask.

"Lead the way," Mr. Sawyer replies. Brooke's dad says very little. When he does talk, everyone listens. It intimidated the crap out of me our first few months of dating.

We head toward the field gate along with many others. Mr. Sawyer nods toward the parking lot. "I'm going to drive Mama and Daddy home. They're waiting in the truck."

Brooke nods.

"You can ride with us, Margaret," Mom offers.

Everyone looks to Mr. Sawyer, as if needing his approval. "Fine by me."

We pile in Mom's van and drive downtown. Half the cars in the county are parked across the street and in the Baptist church parking lot. Mary has music playing and tables set up behind the diner.

So that's how she'll fit everyone.

We park as close as possible to the restaurant. I slide the van door open to the scent of bacon and sweets. People chat in groups and stand in line for what I now see is a buffet.

It doesn't take long for our mothers to disappear with mutual friends, leaving Brooke and me to ours.

"Hey, man," Colt calls from a table nearby.

Brooke and I sit at two empty chairs. Her friend Kristie finds us next, followed by a few more people in our close friend group.

Talk quickly turns to what everyone's doing next. My jaw twitches at the thought that this is getting really real.

We've had awards and scholarship days and my signing. Several people have mentioned college visits and getting accepted places.

But for the first time, it feels real.

Most everyone is going to Apple Cart Community College or somewhere else in the state. Aaron is going to an apprenticeship for air-condition repair. One of Brooke's friends is going into real estate.

One guy got a fishing scholarship to Mississippi State, and

Kyle Tolbert is playing football in college now, but he's a little older.

My mouth goes dry and I cough. It's just minor league, but I don't think anyone from Apple Cart County has played a sport past college. There's a weird responsibility in wanting to represent my town well and not let anyone down.

"Anyone want a drink?" Tiffany comes by holding a cup.

I take it from her and down several gulps before wiping my mouth with the back of my hand. She snarls her nose at me.

"Oh, thanks."

"Um, that was mine." She pokes her thumb over her shoulder. "I was coming to say Mrs. Mary put out more lemonade."

"My bad. Want me to get you a new one?"

She blinks. "I can handle it."

Brooke smirks and bumps my leg under the table. Not my finest moment.

"Nathan Miller."

I turn to several older adults staring at me. Mrs. Ethel is leading the pack as she does most places. She's one of those women who likes to take charge and always knows way too much about everyone.

"I hear you're going to put Apple Cart on the map."

I wrinkle my forehead, unsure what she means.

She pats my shoulder. "That means make us known, son. You know, because you're going to be a famous ball player."

My neck itches and I run a finger under my collar. "It's just minor league, and I may not get to play at first."

She slaps me hard on the shoulder. I flinch, almost spilling my lemonade—or Tiffany's lemonade.

"Don't sell yourself short, kid. We're all counting on you."

The women behind her nod like they've been trained. They're the older version of *Mean Girls*, except nobody's wearing pink.

She pats my shoulder once more, then passes our table. Her followers fall in line. My friends continue talking about summer plans and how odd it is to be done with high school. I halfway listen, but I'm distracted.

All I can think about is how not only is my mom counting on me, but also the whole town.

Brooke

Aaron throws another log on the fire and beats his chest. He earns a few laughs, mostly from a group of tenth-grade girls happy to be able to drive themselves to the field.

Nate rubs my bare arm and hugs me to him. "Do you want to move closer to the fire?"

"I'm good."

He reaches back and grabs a hoodie from the bed of his truck. We're on the tailgate, several feet from the crowd.

"Thanks." I put it on and wrinkle my nose at its strong scent. It's a mixture of four-wheeler gas and hay from sitting out here all night, but I find that pleasantly nostalgic.

Nate leaves in less than a week for Georgia. Some of our friends have already started work or apprenticeships, and even Kristie started two classes at the community college when they began a summer semester.

Part of me wishes I'd started there, but the scholarship to Alabama is something I'd be stupid to pass up. My family can pay for my college, but I don't want them to unless that's the only option.

Maybe leaving Apple Cart for a few years will help shake things up. Get me used to being in the unfamiliar.

Besides, I'll need to get used to traveling if I plan on going to visit Nate.

Colt returns from his truck with a guitar. Several of the younger girls start calling out song requests. One is wearing an Apple Cart County Cheer shirt that the new squad ordered.

I'm a little jealous that I don't own it. Not because it's such a great shirt, but because that means I'm no longer on the squad. One more reminder that I'm fully transitioned into college life.

Colt starts strumming and singing an Eric Church song. I close my eyes and lean back against Nate.

As his voice carries smooth as butter through the summer breeze, I think of Nate. Colt has a great voice and can play the guitar even better. He sings at a lot of local shows and events in town. But he's quick to admit that he's not brave enough to try it for a career.

Nate's the only person I know personally who takes those kind of chances. Most of us are brave when it comes to meaningless things like swinging off a rope at Broken Bridge. Stuff that doesn't matter in life. When it comes to life-changing chances, few of us take them.

The song ends and people clap. I open my eyes to the fire popping and Colt twisting his guitar around his back.

Aaron stands and raises his cup. This should be good.

"Let's make a pact to come back here every week."

Immediately, people start spouting off all they have going on, from family vacations to classes. Aaron frowns and changes his offering to every year.

"We'll try," Nate says.

Every eye turns toward us. I sit up straight and shift at the awkwardness.

"You can come back once a year, dude." I can't decipher if Aaron's tone is more mad or hurt.

"I hope, but I can't make a pact to something that may or may not happen."

Aaron lowers his cup and his eyes.

"I'd love to come here—a lot—but in a few days, I'm no longer in charge of my schedule. I don't know when I'll be where."

Nate's last statement echoes in my head. More reason for me to get used to being away. If we're going to see each other, I need to be the one willing to travel. He will have practices and workouts and games. If I don't have a class, I can study anywhere.

Nate reaches behind him and grabs an empty Mountain Dew bottle from the bed. He lifts it high and grins. "To coming back as soon as possible."

Aaron's face softens. "I'll take it."

Nate nods.

Colt glances at both of his baseball buddies, then adjusts the guitar strap and strums a chord. "Okay, what's next?"

The sophomore girls chatter among themselves, then toss out another request. When Colt starts singing, the mood lightens. Aaron returns to his lawn chair, and everyone carries on as always until curfews begin creeping up on us.

Close to ten, Nate asks if I'm ready to go home. I nod, and we say our goodbyes to everyone. This takes a few minutes, since we all know he might not see some of them again before he leaves.

I try not to get emotional watching the bromance between Nate and his teammates. These boys have played baseball together since we were in elementary school.

Nate wipes the side of his face when we get in the truck. I don't say anything, but I suspect he's emotional too. I've only seen him cry once—at the end of his last high school baseball game. I choose not to ask or mention anything about him leaving and remain quiet for the several minutes it takes to get to my house.

When we go inside, my younger brothers greet us.

"When are you leaving, Nate?" the youngest asks.

"Next week."

Luke nods, satisfied with the answer. He and Austin continue watching TV as if it's no big deal. I know they'll miss Nate too, but they're at the awkward age where they like to look too cool to care.

Nate follows me into the kitchen.

"Want something to drink?"

"Tea is fine."

I grab the orange plastic pitcher that's been in the family longer than me. Mama swears it makes the best tea. That's probably a Southern superstition, but there's also a slim chance some of Memaw's extra sugar stuck to it over the years.

Armed with sweet tea, we enter the sunroom just off the kitchen. All seasons of the year, I enjoy sitting here and staring out the glass walls at the weather. Mama sits here in the morning with her coffee and Bible. It's peaceful then too, but my favorite time is night. Staring at the stars relaxes me, and I can do so without worrying about heat, cold, or bugs.

We sit on a wicker sofa near the edge of the room, perfect for viewing the stars. Nate drapes his arm around me and sighs. "I'm gonna miss this view."

"Yeah, I don't think you can see the stars too well in the city."

"I wasn't talking about the stars."

I turn to Nate smiling at me. "Stop, you're going to make me cry."

He leans closer. "I'm serious. I'll miss sitting next to you, and I'll even miss this place."

"The sunroom?" I joke to keep from tearing up.

"I was meaning more Apple Cart in general, but I've grown pretty fond of this room too." He glances around, then back at me. "We've shared a lot of good talks here. And some good not talks too." He wiggles his eyebrows.

I laugh. Nate dips his head toward mine and kisses me.

I wrap my arms around his neck and get lost in the moment. Next week I can worry about becoming an adult and the complications of a long-distance relationship.

But we've got tonight.

CHAPTER 5

Brooke

"You've got a little something." Nate wipes his thumb across my top lip.

It tickles, and I twist my mouth.

"There." He wipes the frothy residue on a napkin.

Tomorrow, he reports to the team. Tonight, I took him to dinner at his favorite steakhouse in Tuscaloosa. And for once, I refused to let him pay.

Now we're at the coffeehouse we found a few months ago.

"How's your chocolate coffee?"

"Excellent." He follows that with a huge gulp, and shakes his head with his tongue out. "Still a little too hot."

I laugh. "You want to go for a walk?"

"Yeah. Could you show me your dorm?"

"Uh, sure."

I meant go back to Apple Cart and walk between the apple trees like we do sometimes. But it's our last night, so I'll do whatever he wants.

"I need to know where to find it for when I visit."

My face lifts. He hasn't even left yet, and I'm already looking forward to a visit.

We grab our cups and head for the door. "Enjoy the night," the quirky barista calls.

"You too," we answer in unison.

I smile to myself at the memory of our first visit, when he offered us french fries.

We're only a few miles from campus, so it doesn't take us long to park near my dorm. I've been warned about strict parking policies, but hopefully we're safe on a Sunday night in the middle of summer.

Nate climbs out of my car and stretches his legs. No matter how short the drive, he always wants to stretch after being in my Corolla.

"This is it." We stare at a large brick building in front of us. "I'm on the fourth floor."

He cranes his neck. "At the top?"

"Yeah. Daddy wanted me to get a bottom floor at first, thinking it would be safer if there was a fire or something, but those were taken already. Now he's decided the top floor is safer from robberies and such."

"It's got to be hard for him with you moving away."

I snicker. "I'm maybe an hour from home."

"Yeah, but you're the oldest."

"You're the only child."

He nods. "And my mom is taking it about like your dad."

"Want to see inside?"

"Your room?"

"No, silly, it's not my room yet. I mean just the common space."

"Yeah."

We enter the building. Very few people are in the main lobby or the communal room. Nate studies the area as if committing it to memory.

"Want to go back to the orchard now?" I ask.

He smiles. "Lead the way."

The hour it takes to get home feels like both an eternity and a split second.

We talk about anything and everything except him leaving. My mind drifts to that now and again, but for the most part I enjoy the ride.

When we park, I notice a slim shadow lurking around my front porch. Nate puts his hand on my arm before I reach for my door. "Stay here, let me check it out."

I wait nervously as he climbs out and walks toward the figure. About that time, the motion light comes on and the guy lifts his arms.

"Paul!"

That's all I need to hear to know it's safe.

I get out to Paul with his hands lifted, apples at his feet.

"What are you doing here? It's after ten."

He turns to answer me. "Your mom said I could pick apples anytime."

"I don't think she meant now."

He chuckles. "Yeah, daylight would be better."

"As would next month." I point to the ground. "Those apples aren't even ripe."

"Oh." He toes at one with his pointy leather boot.

Nate shakes his head.

"Well, if it's all right with you, then, I'll be back next month."

"Better take that up with my parents."

"Okay." Paul bends and picks up an armful of apples.

Nate and I exchange a look.

He starts walking, then looks at Nate. "Good luck, son. You're always welcome in my store. I'll give you a discount!"

I press my lips together. Considering most of his items are random things he bought at a steep discount, I can't imagine this is much of a deal.

"Thanks, Paul. I appreciate that."

Paul's face lights up. He smiles at us, then forcefully bites a plug from a premature apple. We watch as his face puckers while he chews. He turns and continues walking into the darkness with his bounty.

"Where do you think he parked?" Nate asks after he disappears.

"I'm afraid to ask."

"You think he's done this before at night?"

I shudder. "I'm even more afraid to ask that."

Nate smiles and pulls me toward the front porch. He stops at the top step. "This is my favorite spot around here."

"The porch?"

"Yeah, but this step especially."

"How come?"

A wide grin sweeps across his face. "This is the first place I kissed you."

My lips tingle at the memory. How could I not remember it? We'd had our first date not long after we both turned sixteen. I'd only kissed two other guys, neither of whom I'd cared as much for as Nate.

It's cliché, though accurate, to say he's my first love. And I hope my only—

I hold that thought when his lips fall on mine. He kisses me a few seconds before picking me up to set me on the porch. I giggle against his lips. We have a thing about me standing higher so it's easier for us to kiss.

I come down from my high moment when the porch light blinks several times.

Nate pulls back and sighs. "I know what that means."

"Curfew." I frown.

"It's okay, you can see me in the morning maybe."

"When are you leaving?"

"Like six."

My eyes bug. "Why so early?"

"It's a long drive, and they want me there by noon."

I nod. "Okay."

The lights blink again. I roll my eyes.

"Go, I don't want to get you in trouble."

I give his hand a squeeze and hold it as I back toward the door. When I'm far enough to tug him, Nate drops my hand and blows me a kiss. Then he hurries down the steps to his truck.

Daddy is standing beside the light switch when I come inside. "Just made it," he says.

"Sorry. Nate leaves in the morning."

"You'll see him again."

"He said I could go say bye in the morning at six."

"Fine by me. I'll be working." Daddy sits in his recliner and reaches for the remote.

"Thanks, Daddy." He nods.

I go to the kitchen for some water. Mama meets me in the hallway.

"Hey, honey. Did you hear something weird outside?"

"When?"

"Like maybe ten minutes ago?"

I shake my head. "It was Paul."

"*The* Paul?"

"Yes, ma'am. He was picking apples."

"Late at night in June?" Her voice goes up an octave at the end.

"That's what I asked. He said you told him he could come pick apples anytime."

"That man." Her hands go to her hips as she shakes her head. "I didn't mean anytime, anytime. You'd think he'd have more common sense than that."

"Apparently not." I open my bottle of water.

"Did you have a good night with Nate?"

My bottom lip starts to tremble, so I bite it. Mama reaches out and hugs me, then she talks into my hair. "It's okay, honey. He cares a lot about you. I'm sure he's nervous about you going to college, especially in a co-ed dorm."

"He's not the only one," Daddy calls from the living room.

Mama pulls away from me and frowns at the back of his head. She takes my hand and pulls me toward the kitchen table.

"Ignore your father. He's just overprotective."

Amen to that. I make a mental note to never be that bad when I have a kid.

"What I was trying to say is you shouldn't worry about Nate finding another girl."

My body tenses and I stare at Mama. "I wasn't worried about that . . . until now!"

"Oh, honey." She cups her hand on my cheek and gives it a gentle pat.

"I mean, the thought has crossed my mind, but I've been more worried about not seeing him so much."

"Brooke, every couple goes through times when they see each other less. It may be because of school, or work, or kids. When you three were little, your daddy and I didn't have a lot of time to date and talk, even though we lived together."

"That sounds so sad."

She laughs, then sighs tiredly. "It was worth it to raise you and your brothers."

"And I hope this will be worth it for me to become a teacher and Nate to play professional ball."

"It will. Things have a way of working themselves out."

I force a smile and silently pray she's right. But she usually is . . . she's Mama.

Nate

. . .

My cell phone rings on the dash and I answer. "Hey, Mom."

She's behind me in her van, which is loaded down with whatever my old truck won't carry. Brooke sits beside me and stares out the window. She pulled up at sunrise this morning, and Mom surprised us by saying she'd asked Mrs. Margaret if Brooke could go with us today.

I was pumped to see her and relieved to know Mom wouldn't have to ride back alone.

"Where are we going?"

"Coach said come to the stadium, so follow us."

"Okay." She hangs up.

I return my phone to the dash and pay attention to the GPS instructions. My gut tingles at the notion of moving to a place I've only traveled to twice in my life.

I visited once after my signing, and one time before when our school took an overnight field trip to Atlanta. That was filled with all touristy stuff like the Coca-Cola Museum, the aquarium, and lunch at The Varsity.

The GPS alerts me of an upcoming exit, and I flip on my blinker. I'd driven without one for about year and recently took time to fix it. Brooke urged me to do so before braving Atlanta traffic, and I'm glad now that I listened. I'm used to driving rural roads, with occasional trips to Tuscaloosa.

My truck backfires when we hit the on-ramp. Brooke smirks at me, and I shake my head. Mom's van doesn't look much better from my rearview mirror. "Country's coming to town."

"Nothing wrong with that." Brooke smiles and rests her hand on my knee.

The stadium comes into view with the sun shining behind it. My stomach is a mixture of excitement and fear. I've worked for this since elementary school. Now that it's real, I can hardly believe it.

My gut gets worse when we park and get out. I bend at the waist, afraid the Chick-fil-A I inhaled an hour ago is about to make another appearance.

"Are you okay?" Brooke asks.

I straighten and nod. Mom comes over and shows concern too. I lift my hands. "I'm fine."

They exchange a look, and my face flushes. If anyone can see through my tough exterior, its these two. Luckily, they let it be and don't hound me for a response.

We lock the vehicles and walk through the stadium entrance. Two of the coaches are talking near the field when we enter.

The next hour is a blur as we get an official tour and meet more people with the organization. I've met several before, but Mom and Brooke haven't met any of them.

I try and watch both of them for reactions to everything. As much as they can read me, I can them. Mom appears in awe of everything, and Brooke is wearing her best fake smile. I'm not sure if she's sad or worried.

I choose not to focus on that and worry about my own nerves. That's a full-time job in itself.

We end where it all began. Handshakes and cards are passed out to Mom and Brooke. They both smile genuinely at that, giving me assurance about moving here. The last thing I need is for either of them to worry.

"If you want to unload everything here, we can help get Nate settled into his space," the manager says.

Mom looks to me for an answer. I shrug. "Fine by me."

"It would be nice to get home before dark."

"I can unload your vehicle if you want a moment alone with Nate."

"Thank you." Mom hands him the keys to her van.

That's a sure sign she trusts the man and this organization. She guards the keys to that 2000s-model van like it's a top-secret NASA test unit.

She hugs me and lets out a laundry list of things to watch for and remember. I bite back the urge to say I'm grown and know all of this. Then she kisses my cheek and sniffles. Shockingly, she's not a crying mess. Only a few tears fall, which makes this easier on me.

I turn to Brooke when Mom steps back. "Thanks for coming today."

"Of course, I wouldn't miss it. You'll do great here."

"I hope so." I dip my head and kiss her.

I hope the kiss conveys just how much I'll miss her. I try to hold back on the PDA with Mom and some coaches nearby.

"I'll call you when we're home."

"Thanks." I smile at her pretty face and let out a breath of relief.

We made it through without anyone breaking down. That's a miracle in itself.

Not breaking down is more than I can say for the place I'm living.

Two of the staff members helped haul my belongings to my new apartment. It's a stone's throw from the stadium and about five percent as nice.

I agreed to share this apartment with two teammates sight unseen due to low rent. "You get what you pay for" has never been truer.

Two guys, one of whom I've met briefly once, occupy the couch. They both stand when we open the door.

"Hey, Nate?"

"Yeah." I shake his hand. "Ace, right?"

"Yep, and this is Dominic. He goes by Dom."

Dom stands and shakes my hand. "Welcome."

It's odd looking both of them in the eye, as I've always been the big guy. But we're all big guys here.

"You need help with your stuff?" Dom points to one of the guys bringing in some bags.

"I don't have much. I can probably grab the rest."

"No biggie." Ace taps my chest with his fist.

Both are out the door before I can turn around. They plunder the back of the team SUV and gather the rest of my belongings.

"I guess that takes care of that." The guy who drove everything here laughs.

I follow them up empty handed and a bit guilty for not carrying anything. Now I understand how Mom felt the one time she didn't bring anything to the church potluck.

"Thanks," I say as they drop everything in the living room.

I close the door behind us, and the handle comes off in my hand. "Oh, my bad."

Ace laughs. "It happens more often than you'd think."

"I can fix it if you have some tools."

"For real?" He removes his cap and wipes a hand over bleached hair.

"Yeah."

Dom smirks. "Ace is a city boy, not very handy."

"My tools are a bat and glove," Ace says.

Dom shakes his head. "I have some tools." He stands and walks toward the hallway, then turns around. "It'll be nice to have some help around here."

"Hardy har har," Ace calls behind him.

A water drop falls on my forehead. I glance at the ceiling and another falls.

"It does that sometimes," Ace says.

A dark circle is directly above me on the popcorn ceiling.

"Come on, I'll show you your room."

I follow Ace down the hall, and we squeeze by Dom. He's

digging in an open closet that has a small washer and dryer stacked inside.

"The room on the end is yours."

I enter a room barely large enough for the bed and dresser.

"Perks are it comes furnished." Ace's tone is sarcastic to match his dramatic hand motion.

"As long as there aren't leaks over my bed, it'll be fine." I check the ceiling to be sure. "Lucky for me, I grew up at the lowest end of middle class."

"I see you found your room." Dom sticks his head in the door. I doubt all three of us could fit inside.

"Yep."

"I grew up in the Dominican Republic with seven brothers. You won't hear me complaining," he adds.

"I'm not complaining either," I reply.

Ace laughs. "Be humble if you will. This place is a dump, and we all know it."

"I'm just thankful to be on the team," I counter.

Ace rolls his eyes.

"What?"

"Give it a year," he says. "I'll be in the living room if you need me."

Dom enters and leans against the door frame. "He's disgruntled about getting benched."

I open my mouth to respond but he continues. "It's going to be his third season and things didn't pan out like he expected." Dom steps closer and lowers his voice. "Ace is a good guy, but not used to working for anything. He's from some high society family in Nashville."

I nod. "I can't say I have seven brothers, but I've definitely had to earn my way."

"Yeah, I saw your truck."

We share a laugh. I plop down on my bed, which is springier than I expected. I bounce a time or two and scan my surroundings. It's dry and warm, which is all I need.

"Let me get unpacked and I'll fix that door handle so it will hopefully stay put this time."

Dom smiles. "Tool box is out there waiting on you." He winks and walks out.

I lie back on the bed for a minute and take a deep breath. I gave up a free ride to State for this.

I better make it worth it.

CHAPTER 6

Brooke

Uncle Stewart drives another load of apples into the barn for us to check.

I blow a loose strand of hair from my eyes and make room for them. Erica comes in from carrying another load to the front.

July is our first big harvest month, and it's all hands on deck. My parents and aunt and uncle take total advantage of having kids at their disposal to help. Even more so now that we're older.

Erica joked that next year she plans on taking summer courses, but I can tell she likes being here too. It's part of our roots and family heritage. She wouldn't know what to do without harvest months. Neither would I.

On some subconscious level, I think I leaned toward teaching to have July off for apple picking.

"Galas are looking good this year." Uncle Stewart dismounts the tractor and inspects the apples in the bin.

"Mama said we need at least twenty bags of a dozen up front. People have been calling about them for a week," Erica says.

He shakes his head. "You can't rush God's creation."

I smirk at the memory of Paul picking unripe apples the night before Nate left.

Nate.

I've been extra busy today and haven't thought about him. Is that bad?

Apples roll in front of me on a conveyor belt, calling my attention. I refocus on the task at hand and listen to Erica describe what classes she's taking in the fall.

I'll move into my dorm in a few weeks and start classes soon after. With Nate gone and everyone else going their separate ways to school and work, I'm trying to soak up the only constant in my life: apple-picking season.

Mama comes in wearing her peeling apron, as she affectionally refers to it. She has a peeling apron, a cider-making apron, and a baking apron. We tease her about it, but she swears they help her stay focused on the task at hand.

Maybe I should get a school apron before August.

Hands on her hips, she stops close to Erica and me. "Brooke, do you mind running some apples to town? I'll bring the boys in to help check and bag."

"Sure thing."

I follow Mama to the bakery area, where she spends most of her time. From the outside, nobody would guess that our red barn houses a bakery and store in the front.

Several bushels of apples sit on the countertops. Each one has a tag on the basket with the amount of apples, the price, and who gets it.

"Your dad is taking some larger shipments later to the Pig and Dollar General Market, but Mary and Paul wanted some right away."

I lift my brows. "You mean Paul didn't come pick them himself?"

"Thank goodness, no." Mama rolls her eyes, then laughs.

I carry the bushels one by one to the trunk of my car. Mary ordered four, which means we may see fresh apple pies on the menu soon.

On my last trip to the car, I hear someone yell. I peek around the open trunk to find my brothers at the edge of the field. One is holding a large tree limb, and the other is beside a bucket of apples.

"What are you guys doing?"

They give me a deer-in-the-headlights glare.

"Mama said we could have the bad apples," Austin answers.

"Y'all are going to be the bad apples if you don't get in there and help Erica inspect."

Austin nudges the youngest, Luke, and they head toward the barn. It will be interesting to see how their next ball season goes without Nate here to help. Daddy never played sports as a kid. According to him, aside from being married with kids, his life wasn't much different as a child than now.

Pawpaw even had him driving tractors back then.

I close the trunk and head toward town. Over the next few months, a lot of apples will get shipped to various grocers. Aunt Peggy and Mama will attend farmers' markets and probably host a few tours and field trips.

In the fall, a group of homeschool kids comes to work the orchard one week as part of their science course. They use us to study fruit, and a family in Wisteria who have a hog killing each year to study meat.

I'm not if sure I could stomach being born into that family. I'm still scarred from watching my brothers kill a possum once.

I stop at Paul's store first and snap a selfie with the coffin sign above my head. Then I send it to Kristie. She'll totally cringe, but I think it's hilarious.

Propping his basket on my hip, I open the door with my free hand. A weird noise resembling a duck call squeaks. It stops when I close the door behind me.

Paul's known for having odd gadgets and alarms, and I assume this is a way for him to market whatever it is.

Memaw once bought a plastic pig from this store that oinked when you opened the refrigerator. Her reasoning was to limit Pawpaw's sweet tea consumption. Not even a week later, he took the pig out back and used it for target practice. To my knowledge, she hasn't purchased anything but boots from here since.

"Miss Brooke." Paul slaps his hands together and licks his lips.

"I brought your apples."

"I see."

I set them on the counter, which isn't easy considering all the junk in the way.

"Hang on, dear." Paul slides a rack of sunglasses and slap bracelets to the side, making room.

"Thanks."

"What's the damage?"

I narrow my eyes, not sure what he means.

"How much?"

"Oh, half a bushel, so that's twenty-two dollars."

"'Kay." He opens the register and digs around.

An older man walks up with a dachshund statue that looks like the pet version of a garden gnome. Paul lifts his head and focuses on the fake dog. "You wanna get that?"

"Yes 'er." The man nods.

"Come on." Paul motions him closer.

The man retrieves folded cash from the front pocket of his overalls. He hands it to Paul, who thumbs through it, counting. After a long pause, Paul hands the money to me, then adds a few dollars from the register.

I try to ignore the sweaty texture and shove it in my shorts pocket. "Thanks."

Before anything weirder can happen, I rush to my car and drive to Mary's Diner. I park behind the restaurant and knock on the back door.

One of the waitresses opens it and pops her head out.

"Hey, I have some apples for Mary."

"Four bushels?"

"Yes."

"Great, she's expecting you."

The door shuts, and I blink. It opens a few seconds later to Mary, smiling wide enough to show the slight gap between her two front teeth.

"Hello, child." She wraps me in a hug. "You're a better surprise than the apples."

I laugh. "You want me to bring them through here?"

She lifts a finger and turns her head, then lets out a loud whistle. I jerk, startled.

"Jack, come help Brooke with these apples."

"Yes, ma'am," Jack says as he passes us.

Unlike his best friend, Tanner, Jack has a lot of old-man tendencies and helps with lots of odds and ends around town when he is home from college.

"Jack's helping bake pies today. I have a hunch he'll be quite the cook one day." Mary winks.

I smile, then follow Jack and open my trunk. "They're heavy," I say.

Our bushels weigh over forty pounds. I have to squat to pick up one at a time, and Mama has long since stopped picking them up.

"I got these two." Jack totes a basket under each arm as if it's nothing. He's a lot skinnier than Nate, but definitely as strong.

"I'll get this one."

"Wait, I'm coming back," he calls from behind me.

I shrug and stand by the trunk. Sure enough, he jogs back and gets the last load. Mary meets me at the car with a check made out to the orchard. Unlike Paul, she knew the exact amount. I'm not surprised. They represent both extremes of organization.

"Thanks," I say as I take the check.

"How's our boy Nathan doing?"

"Good, I suppose. He's busy with practices and is helping with a camp to earn extra money."

She shakes her head. "It's a shame these athletes have to choose between getting paid and going to school. I believe one day college athletes will get paid."

I laugh.

"You just wait. See if I ain't right." Mary wags her finger.

"You usually are."

"I pray that boy does well. One day when he's back here, he'll have quite the story to tell. I can imagine him teaching y'all's own kids ball."

"*Our* kids?"

"I'm speaking of the future, sugar."

My chest tightens. It's not like I haven't daydreamed about Nate and me having kids one day. Heck, we've even talked about it a few times. But for someone other than Nate to mention it to me makes it all the more real.

"We'll see," I manage to say with a slight smile.

"Trust me, sugar." Mary pats my arm, then turns toward the restaurant.

I watch her go inside before getting in my car. Despite the ninety-something-degree temperature, I wait a few minutes before cranking my Toyota.

A montage of what could be my future flashes through my mind. Nate is a coach, retired from the MLB. I'm a kindergarten teacher at Apple Cart County Elementary. We have beautiful kids who play between the rows of apple trees like I did as a child.

Maybe Mary will be right.

Nate

"Ugh." I grunt louder and push my arm to its limit.

The ball flies from my fingertips and my foot floats behind me. I suck in a deep breath and come out of my baseball bubble to loud applause.

First year of kid pitch, I trained myself to tune out the background noise and trap myself in an imaginary bubble that can only burst when I toss the ball through it.

Apparently it's still working for me, because the speed meter in the bullpen reads 93.

I shake out my hand as the catcher and one of the coaches approach me. Both grab my shoulder and congratulate me. My face hurts from smiling so big. That's a number I've come close to many times but haven't reached until now.

"Bro!" Dom runs up from the side and hugs me. "Let's go celebrate."

"You still need to catch, Dom."

"Right." He punches my chest lightly. "Later, then."

"Later," I agree.

I'm done for the day and start gathering my gear. They will pair some big-shot pitcher with Dom to give him a run for his money, I'm sure. Hopefully one day, we can start together.

I stop by the locker room for a quick shower. We don't

always have hot water at our apartment, so I'm better off taking one here.

The quick shower drags on as warm water soothes my aching back. Pitching fastballs took everything I had today.

When all the soap is washed down the drain and my hands are wrinkled, I turn off the water and grab a towel. Funny how I once viewed locker rooms as the nastiest places on Earth. Compared to our apartment bathroom, this stadium shower is a five-star resort.

I quickly change into fresh clothes and grab my bag. Something on a nearby bulletin board catches my eye as I leave the stadium.

A Help Wanted sign. It's someone offering twenty-five dollars an hour to have their dog walked. In my current situation, that sounds like a dream job.

Instead of taking a photo of the flyer, I take the whole thing. I don't want any competition for this job; I have enough for my current job. Besides, anyone who can pay twenty-five dollars an hour to walk a dog can afford to print a new poster.

My truck door squeaks when I open it, and I make a mental note to do something about that. I toss my duffel in the seat, then hop in and slam the door. The line "$25 an hour, flexible schedule" stares back at me.

I knew going to the minors I wouldn't make much money . . . but any money is more than nothing. I've heard several guys mention a lawsuit in the works to try and up our pay.

Better not hold my breath for that.

I pull out my phone and dial the number on the poster. It rings several times, and I start to hang up.

"Hello?" a woman answers.

"Hi, ah, yeah. I'm calling about the dog-walking position."

"Yes, it's open."

"Great." I shift in my seat and study the address at the bottom of the paper.

"If you'd like to come talk about it, I'm home now."

"That would be great."

"Come to the address on the ad. Bye-bye."

I raise my eyebrows as she hangs up the phone. It takes me a few minutes to locate the place on my map. Maybe one of these days I'll learn my way around the Atlanta area. Apple Cart was so easy. If you drove around long enough, every dirt road eventually led back to the main highway.

My phone starts calling out directions, adding in turns and traffic lights. As suspected, the route ends at an upscale neighborhood.

I pass the entrance, embarrassed at the way I'm dressed. The job is walking a dog. Still, it's a job, and I should've stopped by my place and changed. At least I did shower.

The map leads to a large Spanish-style home at the end of a cul-de-sac. I climb out, not bothering to lock my door. Nobody in this area would want to rummage through an old pickup.

I travel a concrete line in a perfectly manicured yard and press the doorbell. It rings similar to a bell tower. I step back in case there's an evil villain inside.

I glance around the porch for clues someone sketchy lives here. Maybe I should've brought my bat . . .

The main door opens, but the storm door remains closed. A tiny woman stares at me through the glass. I blink nervously. If looks could kill, I'd be dead and buried by now.

"Hello, I'm Nate Miller. I called about the dog-walking job."

She adjusts her glasses and studies me head to toe, then cautiously opens the other door.

"I'm Gladys. Come in. I had to make sure you weren't an axe murderer first."

I raise one eyebrow. "Do y'all get a lot of those around here?"

She shakes her head and walks slowly toward a living room area. "But if we did, I wouldn't let them in."

I follow and watch her settle into a fancy cushioned chair. This must be the rich people version of a recliner.

"I'm a baseball player, so the only time I chop wood is if my swing is off."

Her face glazes over in confusion, proving my joke fell flat.

"Anyway . . ." I clasp my hands together and smile. "I'm good with animals and would like to walk your dog." I lower myself to sit on the couch across from her.

"You seem like a nice young man, and you're already dressed for walking a dog."

I tug at the end of my gym shorts. That sounded a lot like those backhanded compliments from the women in Apple Cart.

"Let me get Lulu. She makes the final decision."

She sways her weird dress to one side and stands, then shuffles toward a hallway. A few minutes later, I hear a bell. Gladys comes back with the tiniest dog following her. It's wearing some kind of sweater and the bell I hear.

Gladys sits back in her chair, while Lulu thoroughly sniffs my sneakers. She lifts her nose to my ankle, tickling my leg hairs. That's about as tall as she can reach.

She turns toward Gladys, and I relax against the back of the couch, certain this strange test is over. But my relaxation is interrupted by a warm, wet feeling on my toe.

I lean forward to Lulu swatting over my shoe. And that warm, wet feeling? Pee.

I swallow and lift my eyes to Gladys. Her smile covers her whole face. Does she think this is funny?

Before I can say anything, or at least move my foot from the flood, Gladys speaks. "You're hired."

"Excuse me?" That's the last thing I expected to hear after this.

"Lulu only pees on things she likes. Could you start tomorrow?"

"Uh, yes, ma'am. I can get you my practice and workout schedule. Any other time, I'm free."

"Great." She stands and extends her small hand.

I soften my usual handshake since she's old and tiny. She nods, smiles, then bends to pick up Lulu.

Lulu sniffs at me and wags her tail. I reach and pet the dog's fluffy white head. She cocks it to the side.

Between Gladys' axe-murdering evaluation and Lulu's pee approval, I now understand why this job is still available.

But having grown up in a town whose rival school has a cow-poop contest, I think I can handle a five-pound dog relieving itself on my On Clouds.

"I can call you about my schedule when I get to my apartment."

Gladys waves the hand not holding Lulu. "Just text it to me."

My eyes widen. I didn't take Gladys for a texter, but that's not the strangest thing that's happened here. "Yes, ma'am."

She shows me out. I pet Lulu on the head once more, earning another tail wag.

Good thing I own rubber boots.

CHAPTER 7

Brooke

It's bad when you need your phone to find a building. Even worse when you live on campus and have toured the place several times.

I've never been the best with directions, and new construction fences now block the route I planned a week ago. I assume it's illegal to scale a chain-link fence in the middle of town, and I'm wearing a skirt.

In high school, we always dressed nice and cute for the first day. As I pass more and more people in pajama pants and oversized T-shirts, I can see that doesn't carry over into college.

My sandals clap against the sidewalk as I dodge a tree, only to run smack into a skateboarder. My backpack throws me off balance, and I fall. He skates ahead as if he didn't hit a thing. After a few stares and whispers, I realize my legs are apart.

I slap my knees together to close the curtain on my pink-panty show and push myself to standing. That probably cost me a minute or two.

Like a sign from heaven, a stream of light shines on a worn path between a tree line and a building. Almost like a cattle trail. I hurry toward it and notice my map advances on the right path.

Finally. Things are looking up.

That is until I hear thunder. Out of nowhere, a summer shower starts. I run as quickly as possible in my sandals, gripping the strap of my backpack for dear life. I can't be late for my first college class ever.

My feet slide against the soles of my shoes, most likely forming blisters as water pools in them. I cup my hand around my phone screen, thankful for a protective case. Then I silently scold myself for not taking an umbrella.

There were no signs of rain today, but I should know better than to trust Southern summer humidity.

I reach my building and jog up the steps two at a time. Quite the leg workout for a short girl.

People around me take off rain jackets and fold up umbrellas. Others are soaked like me, but don't seem to mind since they're in pajama pants and tennis shoes. I make a mental note to wear shorts and running shoes tomorrow. As well as pack an umbrella.

The building is cold enough to make my teeth chatter, but I've almost made it. I turn down the freshman English hall and step in the first door. I can't believe I made it on time.

I slide in a seat near the door, pull out my notebook, and frown at the moisture across the bottom edge. The professor is busy shuffling papers as a few more people enter. He raises his eyes and starts calling roll, not bothering to introduce himself.

Everyone answers with words I've never heard. I'm so intrigued that it takes a minute for me to realize he never called my name.

I raise my hand and wait for him to notice. My arm feels like a lead pipe as my embarrassment grows every second I hold it up. At last, he points to me.

"You didn't call my name. Brooke Marshall."

He rubs his weird mustache and stares at the sheet. "I don't have a Brooke Marshall."

"English 101?"

"You mean ESL 101?"

ESL. My eyes widen. "I think I'm in the wrong class."

"You need the second door," he responds.

I nod and slide out of the desk. Luckily, I doubt anyone in here picked up on my mistake since they all speak another language.

Sure enough, the label on the door reads "ESL 101." The next door is "ENG 101."

I sigh and tiptoe inside to a plump older man who is already teaching. He narrows his eyes at me but doesn't say anything.

The only empty seat is in front of him. I take it and try not to drown in embarrassment. On the upside, I'm starting to dry.

About ten minutes in, I get comfortable. My clothes are no longer dripping and I'm good at English. Actual English—not learning it from another language.

Things are looking up when my phone rings. The professor raises a bushy brow at me. I fumble for my phone and dismiss the call.

My heart sinks when I see Nate's name across the screen, but I had no choice. I'll have to call him back. I've already gotten two strikes against me in my first-ever college class.

And if anyone understands not wanting to strike out, it's Nate.

The last forty minutes were the longest of my life.

As soon as the class dismissed, I made a beeline for the door. If I speed walk to my dorm, I should have time to change and dry out my hair before the next class.

And call Nate.

I backtrack my cattle trail and hurry down the nearest available sidewalk in the direction of our building. There isn't a cloud in the sky right now, but that doesn't mean I should slow down.

My backpack bounces as I trudge up a hill. The dorm is like a mirage, but I keep pressing until I reach it. Too tired for the stairs, I press the elevator button and try to ignore the girl cutting side eye at me.

The door opens and I lean against the back wall to take some pressure off my soggy feet. I feel the girl watching me when she presses a button. I wait until she's way out of the way to press mine, then return to my post.

She leaves before me, and I kick off my shoes to rub my feet. Yep, I'll definitely have blisters.

The door opens on my floor to several guys and girls holding pizzas. I'm tempted to try and buy one from them but don't want to put forth the effort of fishing out my wallet. It's deep in my pond of a backpack, which also needs to dry.

My keys, however, are in a small side pocket. I access them, no problem, after picking up my shoes and walking barefoot across a very public hallway.

Laughter comes from the other side of the door. I open it to my roommate, snacking on the couch. The laughter is from an old sitcom. I tug my backpack strap up my arm and start toward my room.

"Whoa, why are you wet?"

"I got caught in the rain."

"It's raining?" She stands and opens our blinds.

"Rained."

"Ah. Good thing I don't have class until this evening." She laughs.

"Yeah, lucky you." I half smile and continue to my room.

I didn't meet Ivy officially until orientation. We were matched through the system and connected on social media afterward. She's from a small town like me, but nothing seems to bother her.

Not in a good way like she's super positive. More like an unhealthy level of not caring.

I retreat to my room and peel off my clothes. They've transitioned from soaked to damp to almost dry, but stuck to my skin.

Maybe it's Ivy's nonchalance or the college culture in general rubbing off on me, but I reach for my pajama pants. I'm sure I'll change before going out again, but I see the appeal in midday pajama wear.

I grab my phone and call Nate. It rings a few times. I close my eyes and fall back on my bed. He's probably busy now.

"Brooke."

"Hey." I pop up and settle against the headboard.

"How's your first day going?"

I sigh. "Sorry I couldn't talk before."

"That's fine. I know our schedules are all crazy."

"Yeah. What are you doing right now?"

"Waiting on Lulu to pee."

"Wait, what?" I sit up straighter and wrinkle my forehead.

He laughs. "Lulu is the dog I started walking."

"Why didn't you mention that before?"

He lets out a long breath. "It's embarrassing enough that the dog I'm walking is maybe half the size of a hamburger and wears clothes."

I laugh so hard my side hurts.

"I mean, I need a manly dog like a Lab or Doberman. Even a dachshund."

My cheeks are sore but I laugh even harder. Dachshunds are not manly.

"I miss this." he comments through my laughter.

"What? Walking bigger dogs?"

He chuckles. "Hearing you laugh."

"Me too."

"You haven't been laughing?"

I play with the hem of my pillowcase and twist my lips. "Today was a little stressful."

"I'm sorry."

"No, it's fine." I toss the pillow and lie back. "I have two afternoon classes that are sure to go better."

"What happened?"

What didn't happen? "Let's just say running around construction zones, then getting stuck in a rainstorm. That led to me rushing to the wrong class, where they were teaching English to foreign students . . ."

Now it's Nate's turn to laugh. I sigh. "I miss your laugh, too."

"Yeah, maybe someday soon we can laugh together in the same room."

"That would be perfect." I close my eyes and imagine him beside me.

"Soon as I get enough of a break to see you, I'm coming. Tuscaloosa, Apple Cart, wherever."

"Can't come soon enough."

"Come on, Lulu."

I smile at the image of Nate talking to a tiny dog. He's always patient and would be the best dad someday.

"Hey, I'm taking her back to Gladys. Text me after your last class and let me know how it went."

"Will do."

"Love you, Brooke."

"I love you, too."

I hang up the phone and stare at the screen. It's a photo of us from graduation. The one where we're no longer wearing our caps and gowns. That's the last photo we took together, which seems symbolic of how things are changing.

Hopefully I can take a new photo of us soon.

Nate

She licks my lips before I can stop her.

I wince and hand Lulu to Gladys, who cackles loudly as she takes the tiny dog.

"I see you two have reached a level beyond peeing."

I frown. "I think I preferred the peeing."

Gladys laughs even louder and flaps her free arm. Lulu looks at her owner as if wondering when the laughter will stop. I imagine it's even more annoying to a dog's ears.

"Okay." Gladys sighs. "Hang on, let me pay you."

She disappears into the house. I wait on the porch until she returns with some cash.

"Here's your money for the week."

"Thank you." I smile.

"You're welcome. I let Lulu rest on the weekends. I'll be in touch with you Monday."

"Sounds good." I turn and retreat to my truck.

As I fold the bills in my wallet, my phone dings. It's Dom.

What are you doing?

> Getting off work.

I haven't revealed to my teammates that "work" means walking a tiny dog around a ritzy neighborhood.

> We're going to Pool Pub if you want to come.

I thumb through the money Gladys gave me. There's enough for a good meal and gas.

> Sure. Text me the address.

I open my maps and punch in the address. I'm not much for playing pool, or going to bars, but I've heard they have great burgers.

My stomach growls at the thought of eating something other than ramen noodles and Doritos. If I didn't put so much time in practicing and trying to prove my worth here, I'd get a second side job.

The lowering sun blinks between the trees lining Gladys's neighborhood. I reach for my sunglasses and follow the directions to the interstate.

When I exit again, it's in a much less affluent place. One where my truck will fit in—and possibly get broken into. But I wouldn't expect much more from a place known for burgers, beer, and pool.

Dom's old SUV sits out front. Smart move not taking

Ace's new truck. I park as close as possible to him and lock everything.

Old country music echoes from inside before I open the door. A group of smokers hang to one side. I hold my breath and hurry toward the back. Two pool tables surrounded by dinner tables face a small stage.

Ace spots me first and waves me over. He's holding a pool stick in his other hand.

I slide past a few couples dancing and sit in a chair near Dom. He's sipping on a Coke while Ace plays pool with a woman.

"Isn't she a little old for him?" I ask Dom.

The woman across the pool table could easily pass for forty. She's attractive and slim, but in a very mature and could-be-our-mom kind of way. Not someone who should flirt with college-aged kids.

"Ace has a thing for older women."

"How old?"

Dom laughs. He leans closer to talk over the jukebox.

Yep, there's a literal jukebox by the stage. I suppose they do live music or maybe karaoke sometimes, but tonight it's empty.

"The waitress will be back in a minute. I told her I'd wait on you to order."

"Cool."

A woman maybe a little older than us comes up and smiles. "I see your date is here."

Dom and I exchange a glance. He leans away and scoots his chair farther back.

"We're just friends," I say, trying not to laugh.

"Okay, I apologize." She blushes.

I lift my hands. "It's fine, really." I'd hate to embarrass her further.

"What can I get you to drink?" She places a menu on the table in front of me, then another in front of Dom.

"Sweet tea." I scan the menu. They have quite the selection of burgers for a small hole-in-the-wall place. I find something with bacon and extra cheese. "I'll have the Baconator."

"Excellent selection," she says.

"Queso burger with onion rings instead of fries," Dom adds.

"Got it." She takes up the menus. "Will that be one ticket or two?"

"Two," we say in unison.

Dom scoots his chair even farther from me. So far back that he bumps into a girl, causing her to spill her drink. She shrieks.

"My bad." He jumps up and grabs the roll of paper towels off our table.

Instead of breaking off a towel, he runs the entire roll down the girl's shirt. Probably for the best since he splashed her front.

She winces and grabs the roll from his hands. Then she hurries off. Dom drops his head in his hands and groans.

I pat him on the back . . . just in time for the waitress to show up with our drinks.

She sets them in front of us and smirks at me. Thankfully, Dom's head is still down. I drop my hand from his shoulder and grab my tea. He slowly lifts his head and returns to normal when he doesn't see the girl around.

"Dude, you were killing it this morning at practice!"

"Thanks." I sip my tea. "You weren't half-bad yourself."

He laughs and nods. I follow his eyes to Ace, who's standing awfully close to the older woman. She's hanging on his every word. "You don't think he'll go out with her, do you?"

Dom shrugs. "You never can tell with Ace."

I raise a brow, and Dom laughs again.

"Don't worry. He never brings them back to the apartment. At least not since we've roomed together."

I lift my chin. "Good to know."

"You working this weekend?"

I shake my head.

"I gotta go in tomorrow." Dom helps detail cars for extra money, mostly on the weekends.

"Ace is lucky to not need the money."

Dom sighs. "Ehh."

"What do you mean, 'ehh'?"

He chugs his drink, then points to Ace. "He will never know what it's like to work for something."

I cock my head and watch Ace closer. He's a good ballplayer from a wealthy family. The only reason he's living with us is because his dad gives him an allowance that he prefers to waste on his vehicle and going out rather than on a nice apartment.

I turn to Dom. "He has to work for his position on the team."

He nods. "That he does, and it bothers him way worse than it does us, trust me."

"Yeah?"

"We were all the best at high-school level or we wouldn't be here. But we still worked our tails off. Is there anything you've ever gotten easy?"

"Brooke," I whisper.

"Huh?" Dom leans closer to hear me over the music.

Of course, the waitress chooses that very moment to bring our burgers. "I hate to interrupt," she says.

Dom moans and takes his plate. "Thanks." He doesn't even bother to explain this time, and I find it comical at this point.

When she walks away, Dom turns to me. "What?" he asks louder.

"I said Brooke."

"What about Brooke?"

"You asked is there anything I've ever gotten easy. Brooke

and I just kind of clicked. We hit it off, and ever since our first date, never wanted to be apart."

"Good for you, man."

I grunt.

"That's not good?"

"Now we're apart."

"Yeah, man, but you're working and she's in school."

"Yeah, but not right this second. I don't have work or practice for two days. If I leave right now, I could be there in a few hours."

I stand. Dom stares at me. "What about your burger?"

I toss a hard-earned twenty on the table.

"Can I eat it, then?" He licks his lips at my plate.

"No, bro. I paid for this. I'm taking it to-go." I down the rest of my tea, then pick up my plate. "Thanks for the invite. See you Sunday."

Dom's mouth drops as I march toward the exit. I'm in my truck headed down the road before I realize I took a real plate with me. Oh well, good thing I left a nice tip.

Tuscaloosa, here I come.

CHAPTER 8

Nate

I polish off my burger at a red light. After balancing a breakable plate on my knees in traffic, I have a new appreciation for to-go boxes.

No wonder Paul is obsessed with them.

I turn on my headlights and exit onto the interstate. There's an equal amount of people traveling both ways. I fall in line and settle in for the long ride.

The radio is usually a good distraction, but every song that plays reminds me of Brooke. When a commercial comes on for a farmers' market, I think of her family's orchard and turn it off.

My mind is so fixated on her that I'm almost to Tuscaloosa when I notice my gas light. There's no special ding or reminder in my old truck other than the light that sometimes works.

Even if it's on, I still have to check the gauge. The light sometimes has a mind of its own.

Yep, the gauge is on E.

At least my blinkers work well. I put the right one on and shift to the far right lane. Two eighteen-wheelers sandwich me in for about a mile before I can exit at the nearest gas station. And both trucks exit with me. I manage to slide away when they veer toward the diesel fuel.

My truck sputters a little when I pull up to the pump.

Thanks to Gladys, I have more cash than money on my card. Since most places in Atlanta prefer cards, I save my card money and choose to pay inside.

Big mistake. There's a line of people waiting at the register.

I shove my hands in my pockets and bounce on the balls of my feet at the back of the line. Two kids ahead of me fight over a bag of chips. The mom snatches it from their hands, ripping a hole in the bag.

She sets the bag on the shelf as if nothing happened.

I stare at some chips beside my shoe. *Should I pick these up?*

"What?" the woman asks accusingly when I lift my head.

I shrug and turn my gaze to the refrigerators. I keep staring that way as the line moves up and try to ignore the chips crunching under my feet.

The woman eventually leaves the line, dragging a kid with each hand. That jumps me ahead one space. I'm now close enough to witness the current customer asking to see various cigarette boxes before he makes a selection.

I don't know a lot of smokers, but always assumed they just smoked the same stuff. Like how people either prefer Pepsi or Coke.

This could be the guy's first time smoking. Though I seriously doubt it, since he could pass for seventy and sounds like he swallowed a bullfrog.

He settles for the unfiltered variety of some brand I've never heard of and checks out.

We all move up, and I'm next in line. The woman ahead of

me buys a scratch-off ticket, which I thought was illegal in Alabama. She scratches it quickly with a long red fingernail, then buys another.

This goes on for about five minutes straight.

I take off my cap and run my hand over my face and hair, trying to have patience. Eventually she will run out of money, or the store will run out of tickets.

As suspected, the first happens in another minute. She drops her shoulders and leaves, about twenty dollars in the hole, with a scuffed nail.

"Hi, I need twenty dollars on pump two."

I slide a twenty through the slit in the window. There's a barrier of glass separating me from the cashier. Kind of like at a movie theater, but in a much sketchier way because it also has metal bars and is lined with Slim Jims.

The guy grabs my money like he's playing slapjack, then nods his head. We stare at each other a second before someone behind me grunts loudly. That's my cue to leave.

I hurry out and fill my truck, anxious to get back on the road. I'm beginning to see why Atlanta businesses prefer cards.

A Cracker Barrel sign welcomes me back to the interstate. The photo includes a big slice of apple pie, which I accept as a literal sign I'm on the right path. Also, it says "Tuscaloosa" at the bottom.

A few short miles later, I exit toward McFarland Boulevard. I'll be at her dorm in less than a half hour. I shift in my seat, tired from the long drive and anticipation of seeing Brooke.

My heartbeat picks up a notch with every traffic light. I'm close enough to see exit signs to the university. Just in time for my truck to sputter.

I slow down and pull into the right lane. Vehicles whiz by, and I realize how much I actually slowed. The gas doesn't seem to work, and I know enough from tinkering with old vehicles to know something is wrong. I turn the wheel and veer into the ditch not far from my exit.

Everything under the hood appears fine. At least what I can tell from the streetlights and using my phone as a flashlight. Something smells odd, and I don't think it's the fast food places across the road. I sniff near the gas tank and wince.

Dang it. That sketch place sold me bad gas.

I straighten my cap and shut the hood. There's a Texaco sign on the hill, lit like the Christmas star offering hope.

I rummage through my toolbox and find a gas can. If I can somehow siphon out the bad gas and replace it, I can drive.

In what I hope is a wise-man decision, I follow the Texaco star and fill my canister at the pump. I use my card, even though this place doesn't look overrun by fighting families and smokers trying to strike it rich with dollar tickets.

With no auto-parts store nearby and my limited resources, I'm forced to redneck engineer this gas switch.

There isn't any kind of hose in the back of my truck, so I pop the hood and unhook the wiper-fluid line. Not ideal, but I need gas more than wiper fluid right now.

When I'm done dumping the bad gas and about to add the new, a car honks. I jump about three feet and angle toward the road, where I can better see the traffic.

I fill the truck quickly as possible, then return the tube to its rightful place. It cranks for the Texaco gas, and I'm back in business.

Brooke's dorm is a few blocks away. My legs are cramped and I'm pretty sure there's poison on my tongue, but it's all about to be worth it.

Every free spot I try and park in has some kind of code indicating it's for faculty and staff or a resident. I wind in and out of side roads and end up a decent hike from her dorm. But hey, I'm here.

The day we visited it together comes to mind as I enter the

building. I hurry to the elevator, which takes forever. The door opens to a girl holding a lizard in a fish tank. I blink, although I shouldn't be too surprised with the way this trip has gone.

I punch the number for Brooke's floor and stare at the ceiling. It dings and the door opens.

The girl gets out with her lizard, and I follow. I crane my neck at all the closed doors to check their numbers. I'm coming up on Brooke's door when lizard girl stops.

I bump into her, causing her to drop the aquarium. She gasps, and the lizard crawls down the hall.

"I'll get him!" I sprint toward the scaly thing that's a lot faster than he looks.

"He's a she," the girl calls out behind me.

Like that matters right now.

The lizard turns toward an open door. I leap and catch his —or her—tail right as she enters the room. Screams come from inside as I fight to get a better grip on it.

I squeeze its backside and pull it toward me. Two girls sit on a couch, legs curled under them.

"Sorry." I manage to stand and tug the lizard toward me so I can close the door with my free hand.

Its owner meets me halfway down the hall, holding the aquarium. I set the thing inside and wipe my hands down my pants. It hisses at me before she can secure the lid.

"Thanks," she says.

I nod, then head toward Brooke's door. The girl stops beside me. "Are you looking for something?"

"This is Brooke Marshall's room, right?"

She half smiles and opens the door. I'm not sure what she means until she fans her hand for me to enter.

I do so cautiously in case this is some kind of voodoo that lizard princess prepared to cast a spell on me for squeezing her pet.

I may not be able to outsmart her, but I can probably

outrun her. That's the plan I make in my head before turning to a closed door with "Brooke" plastered on a sunflower door hanger.

My mood lifts, and a jolt of adrenaline returns, making this whole ordeal worth it.

Lizard girl must be the weird roommate she told me about. Good thing I returned the lizard in one piece.

After two quick knocks, the door opens, and Brooke jumps into my arms. When she puts her lips on mine, all the trouble is worth it.

Brooke

Of all the things I expected to find on the other side of my door, Nate wasn't one of them.

Not that I'm disappointed.

I kiss him like I haven't seen him in a year, when it's really been ten days. But it seems like a year while I'm away from everything familiar, trying to maneuver around a campus my hometown could fit in three times over. Minus all the farmland and timberland, of course.

After a long while, I pull back and smack my lips. "Why do you taste like rubbing alcohol mixed with gasoline?"

He winces and rubs his face, which hasn't been shaved in a while. "And here I was worried about my facial hair being a bother."

I laugh and rub his chin. "I kinda like it. You have a more mature look."

He grins. "I guess I've been shaving all this time for you."

His grin fades. "And I had to siphon gas with a wiper-fluid tube."

My eyes bug. "Oh dear. Come on." I pull him into my bathroom and find an extra toothbrush and some mouthwash.

"Is it *that* bad?"

I wrinkle my nose.

"My bad."

"Still worth a great, long kiss." I wink, and he laughs.

"I missed you." He kisses the top of my head, then grabs the toothbrush.

"So what led to you siphoning gas?"

Nate points to the toothbrush in his mouth with his free hand. I nod and wait for him to answer. He spits, rinses, and wipes his mouth with the back of his hand. "Gah, that's better." He holds the toothbrush out. "I'd burn this."

I smirk. "It's fine."

I pluck the brush from his hand and set it in the holder next to mine. Maybe he can visit more often and use it again.

"Back to siphoning gas . . ."

He shakes his head. "It's a long story."

I take his hand and lead him back to my room. We sit on the edge of my twin bed. He bounces a few times and stares at the bed funny. "Why is this so high?"

"They elevate the beds to make storage room beneath." I lift the cover beneath my dangling feet to show the storage bins I have under it. "Ivy has her bed so high that there's a desk under it."

"Sounds dangerous."

"Yeah, well, she's a bit dangerous at times."

"No kidding. I met the lizard."

"Oh, you met Camy. She's a chameleon."

"Ivy got on the elevator with it, then the thing got loose in the hall and I had to chase it down."

I scrunch my nose. "Camy is fast. That's why I keep my doors shut."

"I'm surprised they allow her to have it."

I sigh. "She somehow convinced the RA that it's an evolved fish."

He frowns and I laugh. "So gas?"

"That happened before Camy. I bought a bad batch at some ghetto gas station off the interstate and it stalled my truck. I made it close to the college exit and got better gas at a Texaco."

"And you siphoned it with the wiper tube?"

"Yep."

"Why didn't you call me if you were that close?"

"That would ruin the surprise of me coming."

I roll my eyes.

"Seriously." He wraps his arms around me. "I wanted to surprise you."

I lean on his shoulder, suddenly aware that we're alone on my bed. My neck and chest heat up.

This would never be allowed at my parents' house, and it isn't a situation I'd put myself in under normal circumstances. But this is the only room other than my bathroom that isn't the public domain of a fast and unfriendly reptile.

"You want to go for a walk?"

Nate pulls back and blinks with confusion.

It's dark outside and the humidity is still beach-level.

"Sure?"

I smile and hop off the bed. Before he can stand, I'm digging in a storage bin for tennis shoes.

"We can get some ice cream. My treat," I say casually.

"Yeah, I could go for that." He stands and straightens.

I smile up at him from the floor as I pull on my last shoe. He reaches for my hand and helps me to my feet.

My face flushes as he pulls me close. I hurry toward the

door, embarrassed that I'm feeling this way. Maybe it will wear off the longer he's here.

In all the time we've been dating, I haven't gone more than a week without seeing Nate until now. That's got to be it.

Sadly, I best get used to not seeing him as often.

He wraps his arm around my shoulder after I close the door behind us. I can't give Camy free rein in my room. Once I found her hiding in my shoe and almost peed myself.

I'm a few weeks into my first semester and already counting down the days when I can move out of the dorms. We lived just far enough away for the school to not allow me to live at home. Also, Mama said it would be good for me to leave Apple Cart for a bit, even if I plan on coming back after college.

She's most likely right. But I'd love to be watching the stars from our sunroom about now. Instead, I'm off to find ice cream as an excuse to escape quarantining in temptation while we avoid a lizard.

"Does Camy roam around your dorm?" Nate asks when we're on the elevator.

"Not a lot. Ivy claims she needs so much exercise to stretch. The problem is that she's so fast, it's hard to catch her when she's out."

"Maybe she needs a bigger aquarium."

"Good idea."

He twists his mouth. I study his jawline, half hidden by the stubble. His facial hair is starting to grow on me.

"Why did she have it on the elevator?"

"Vet checkup."

Nate frowns and shakes his head. I laugh.

"There's a good place near the strip, but it may be crowded."

"That's fine if it's what you want. We're off tomorrow, so I can stay as long as you'll let me."

He smiles at me and I swallow. I consider asking him to

stay indefinitely, but that would be selfish of me. Even as a joke.

I didn't realize how hard the distance would be for me. Nate has traveled a decent amount for ball the past few years. However, it was always a few days here and there for a tournament. Often they were close enough where I could go watch. He practiced locally, too.

There's a good chance he'd have been just as busy had he chosen to play college ball. It's something I need to accept. I can't hold him back from his dreams, as he wouldn't me from mine.

"You're awful quiet."

"Hmm?" I stop and turn to Nate.

He brushes his hand across my cheek and through my hair, then kisses me gently on the temple.

"I'm just soaking in us being here together," I lie.

That sounds much more appropriate than admitting I'm already dreading him leaving. Nobody wants to come off as the obsessive girlfriend who can't do life apart from her guy.

"Is this it?"

"Yep." We take the sidewalk toward a huge ice cream cone sign. It's not as crowded as I expected. Then again, it's an away game for football. If the game were here, we couldn't get in anywhere quickly.

It takes us longer to decide on flavors than it does to get our order.

We walk around slowly with cones stuffed full of Blue Bell. The conversation covers everything from our families and friends to his roommates and the infamous Lulu, who we both agree is better than Camy.

Nate finishes the last bite of his cone and stretches.

"Want mine?" I hold out the half cone I have left.

"Of course." He grins and takes a big bite.

I glance around the quad, trying to think of somewhere

else we can go. Aside from the library or heading toward town, I'm at a loss.

"Want to go watch a movie on Netflix?"

"Anything that lets me rest my legs after driving and walking so much."

Guilt washes through me. *Why did I make him walk around so much?*

"Of course, you should've said something."

"Nah, it's good. The weather is nice. I worked out a lot yesterday, then walked Lulu earlier before driving."

I nod and smile as we turn toward my dorm.

Maybe his breath still tastes like gasoline and wiper fluid. I need all the restraint I can get.

CHAPTER 9

Brooke

The sun shines through my blinds, and I roll over toward the wall.

Except Nate is between me and the wall.

I flinch and roll so fast the opposite direction that I fall off the bed.

He snores a little, which is good and bad. Good in the sense that I didn't wake him. Bad in the sense that if he snores at this age, how bad will it get when we're in our twenties and married?

I shake my head and try not to think about marriage and all that.

He wasn't supposed to stay all night, but he did. And I still don't get how we both fit in that tiny bed.

My heart pounds as I ease to my feet and tug at my T-shirt. It's actually his T-shirt, or old T-shirt. One he used to practice in but is now worn out. I like that it's thin and soft. Not so useful for baseball, but perfect for lounging. It covers my running shorts, making me more self-conscious about him still being here.

If my parents knew he stayed all night, they'd have my hide.

He snores again, jerking my attention off my ragged appearance. I pull my hair back with the hair tie on my wrist and take a deep breath.

Should I wake him or let him sleep? Do I go make breakfast? Maybe I should stay in here until I know if Ivy is gone.

She works at a bookstore on campus, and I'm pretty sure she's working this weekend.

Weekend.

I tiptoe to my desk and grab my phone. No missed calls or texts.

I sit in the desk chair and sigh. Mama is expecting me to come home for church tomorrow morning, but I didn't say when I was coming. Last weekend I drove home Friday night. I hope she isn't worried.

Nate snores again.

I take that as a warning not to call Mama. She might sense he's here.

How old do you need to be to not worry about what your mama thinks? Apparently, it isn't eighteen and a half. At least not for me.

I yawn widely and check the time on my phone. It's not even six. No wonder I'm still tired.

Snuggling with the throw I keep on my desk chair doesn't help, so I move to the floor. More like the brick surface disguised by cheap carpet.

After several minutes of wiggling and wishing Nate weren't wrapped in all the good covers and both my pillows, I stand.

I already feel like someone is spying on us in here together, but I need sleep.

Tired as I am, I have a grand idea. Okay, maybe not grand, but pretty good for six in the morning.

I sneak toward the bed and squeeze next to him, except my feet are by his head and my head is by his feet. The way horses stand in a pasture.

As an added bonus, the snoring isn't so loud from this angle. I wiggle my face away from his feet and turn my head. That's the last thing I remember before dozing off.

I'm well rested by the time weird music plays loudly by my head. Well, as rested as I can be sharing a twin bed with a huge guy whose toes are hooked in my hair.

I twist to cover my face with the blanket, when Nate kicks me in the face.

"Ouch!"

He shoots up in the bed to me holding my throbbing nose.

"Sorry. Are you okay?"

He holds the back of my head and tries to see my face. I allow him to tilt my head back. "Your nose isn't bleeding."

The music blares again.

"You can turn that off. It's my alarm."

I lean toward my desk and grab his phone. It's nine o'clock.

"You need an alarm for nine?"

"Sometimes." He crawls to my end of the bed and sits beside me. "How's your nose now?"

"Throbbing less."

He kisses the tip of it.

"Better." I smirk.

He kisses beside my nose, then kisses the corner of my mouth. My smile widens as he kisses me square on the lips.

I pull back after a minute, and he stares at me. "My bad. I need to brush my teeth."

My cheeks flush. "Me too."

I play it off like morning breath is the problem. If only that were the worst of our problems.

He hops off the bed and stretches. I follow him to the bathroom, noticing that Ivy isn't around. We stand on either side of my sink, brushing our teeth.

I don't know if I can get used to not seeing Nate for long periods of time, then having him stay here. I'm not sure if that's good for either of us.

A million sentences form in my head on how I should start this conversation. But how would it end? Would we agree to meet up in Apple Cart all the time, even though Tuscaloosa is closer to Atlanta? Or . . .

I swallow so hard, I choke on toothpaste.

Breakup has never been in my vocabulary. Nate has been my only serious relationship, and I plan on keeping it that way.

I rinse my mouth and take a deep breath. We need to set some ground rules and figure out how to be long distance and stay the same.

"Where were we?" Nate tosses his toothbrush in the sink and kisses me. My brain goes to mush and my toes curl.

I definitely do not want to break up. Whatever we have to talk about can wait until after this kiss, or even later.

Actions really do speak louder than words.

Nate

It's close to eleven when I walk out of Brooke's dorm.

The sun beats down as I lead her to my truck.

"You're sure the truck is fine to drive to Atlanta?"

"Yeah. I got all the bad gas out."

She smiles, and I open her door.

"Oh." She hands me the plate from the restaurant. "What's this?"

I laugh and set it on the dash. After I shut her door and get in, I explain how I took my burger to-go without a to-go box. By the time I get to the part about me balancing the plate on my knees at a red light, we're both laughing.

"Turn here." Brook points to a road ahead.

We agreed to go to the coffee shop we found this summer. This weekend has been one of the best of my life, and I want a big chocolate coffee to top it off.

I wish I were in a better location for her to visit me too, since her schedule is more stable. Something about her driving to Atlanta alone and navigating my neighborhood doesn't sit well with me.

Even worse, what if she stopped somewhere and got bad gas?

I could never forgive myself if something happened to Brooke on her way to visit me. I'll just have to make it a priority to visit her whenever I can.

Maybe one day I can afford to live in a better location. And maybe after that, I can afford to buy her a ring.

I park in front of the coffee shop and wait on her to get out. It's still pretty busy for almost lunchtime. The chalkboard outside advertises a chocolate pastry that sounds good.

We wait to the side as a group of people exit, then we go in. The scent of coffee hits my nose, and I can almost taste the chocolate.

Part of me panics for a split second that they no longer serve chocolate coffee. But it's still on the menu behind the counter. I order that and a chocolate pastry, then wait for Brooke to order.

"That's a lot of chocolate," she comments as we find a table.

"I'm very hungry."

"When are you not hungry?"

"Good point." I grin.

They call our number and I stand to pick it up. Brooke's cheeks are pink and her hair is pulled back from her face. I study her and commit every detail to memory.

Her big brown eyes, long dark hair, soft skin. I miss her already.

I sit across from her and slide our tray on the table. She takes her coffee and blows it lightly. Puckering her lips tempts me to kiss her, but I won't here in the coffee shop.

"Are you headed back to Atlanta after this?"

"Yeah. I don't have time to visit with Mom, so it's best not to tell her I'm so close."

She frowns. "You could've left earlier and visited her."

"I'm where I want to be." I reach across the table for her hand. "I feel most at home when I'm with you."

Her eyes soften and she blushes. "That is so sweet."

"Yeah, maybe don't repeat that I said that." I wince.

"Why?"

"It does sound really Hallmark when I say it aloud."

She laughs, then takes a sip of her coffee. I bite into the chocolate square that is every bit as delicious as the chocolate drink. "Man, this is good."

"Want some of my blueberry?" Brooke smirks when she asks. She knows I'm not a fan of blueberry.

"I'm good."

We finish our food and talk a little more before driving back to her dorm. Knowing I won't be here much longer, I park closer to the entrance. "It's quiet here this weekend."

"Told you. No football game. It's a totally different campus."

"Yeah." I stare at the almost empty street in front of her dorm. "I wish I could just take you with me."

Her face softens. "I know. It's been harder than I thought. I keep hoping the more we get used to this, the better it will be."

I cup her face and bring her in for a deep kiss. She sighs against me when it ends. I hug her close.

After a few minutes, she mumbles, "I need to go pack."

She texted her mom that she would be home sometime today, and we both know her mom will worry if she doesn't make it before dark.

"I know." I pull back and stare into her eyes. "I'll go and help you carry down your bags."

She nods and leans back. Her elbow hits the plate I shoved between the seats. "Oh, here." She hands me the plate.

"I may as well throw this out. It would look stupid to return it now, and I did leave a good tip." I take it and turn it over in my hand.

"I've got an idea." She takes it back and opens her door.

Instead of asking, I follow her inside and up the elevator to her room. She hugs the plate close as we walk to her dorm.

When we enter, she goes straight to her desk and pulls out a Sharpie. She scribbles something on the plate, then goes to the bathroom with it.

I stand between her room and bathroom, trying to figure out what she's doing.

"Here."

I take the plate and hold it up. A big kiss mark is at the bottom in her lipstick color. Above it she wrote "Brooke's Home Plate."

My cheeks hurt from smiling. I love a good pun.

"What's this for?" I smile at her.

"You said being with me felt like home. This is a plate, so I made it a home plate. Whenever you miss me, look at this and you'll have a kiss from me."

I pull her close and kiss her. Who knew a plate from a burger joint could become so valuable?

We back against the wall, still kissing. I know we're up here to pack her for Apple Cart, but I have to get in one last kiss.

And whatever my future holds, I pray it includes this girl. She truly is my home.

Welcome to the Coffee Loft, a place where romance is always brewing . . .

Grab your favorite table over in the corner and be prepared to be swept off your feet. This multi-author collection features some of your favorite sweet romance authors that you already know and love as well as a few new names you'll be rushing to check out. From cold brews to cappuccinos and frothy frappes, there's something on the menu for every romantic comedy reader. Fake dates, meddling matchmakers, friends-to-lovers and so much more, each stand-alone story is the right blend of sweetness, guaranteed to warm your heart. Happily-ever-afters coming right up!

Series link: https://books.bookfunnel.com/thecoffeeloftseries

Want to see what takes place eight years later between Brooke and Nate?
Sign up for Kaci Lane's newsletter and get the first scene from *Mom Ball*.

ACKNOWLEDGMENTS

First, I'd like to thank God for giving me creative ideas and placing the right people in my path to help see them to fruition.

My husband, Blake, gets credit next for always supporting my writing endeavors, even if he finds my stories a little too "girly and Hallmarkish." Of course, this book kind of broke the mold when it comes to that.

I also want to thank my readers and ARC team for their support. It means the world to me that busy people would give of their time to read early, post reviews, and share the news of my books with their friends. I couldn't do this without y'all!

As always, I'd like to thank my editor, Joanne, and my proofreader, Charity. Both of these ladies are huge help to making my books shine!

ABOUT THE AUTHOR

Kaci Lane is a journalist turned fiction writer who believes all stories should have a happy ending. While unsuccessfully trying to learn Spanish for a decade, she has become fluent in sarcasm, Southern belle and movie quotes. She is married to a Southern Gentleman and has two young children who help keep her humility in check. Connect with her on kacilane.com or Facebook.

BOOKS BY KACI LANE

For exclusive deals, check out kacilanebooks.com.

Single Southern Mamas Series*

Mom Squad

Mom Ball (Coming Summer 2024)

Mom Bod (Pub date TBD)

Bama Boys Series*

Hunting for Love

Chicken about Love

Hammered by Love

Cutting out Love

Geared for Love

Guilty of Love (Pub date TBD)

Apple Cart County Christmas*

Christmas in Dixie

Crazy Rich Rednecks

Queen of My Double-Wide Trailer (coming soon)

Schooled on Love Series

Taco Truck Takedown

Side Hustle

Buggy List

Off-Season

Books in Shared Series with Other Authors

The Coffee Loft

No Time for Traditions

A Perfect Match in Silver Leaf Falls

*If you enjoyed spending time in Apple Cart County, revisit your favorite Southern community with these series. Check them out on my website.

www.ingramcontent.com/pod-product-compliance
Lightning Source LLC
LaVergne TN
LVHW092055060526
838201LV00047B/1395